A LETTER FROM THE
COLONIAL WILLIAMSBURG
FOUNDATION

John Nicholas was a real boy who lived in Williamsburg, Virginia, in the 1770s. His father, Robert Carter Nicholas, was a member of the House of Burgesses and treasurer of the Virginia colony. The Nicholases were part of the gentry, the wealthiest two percent of residents in eighteenth-century Virginia.

Today, Colonial Williamsburg is a living history museum. Colonial Williamsburg's Historic Area has been restored to look the way it did at the time of the American Revolution. People in costume tell the story of Virginia's contribution to American independence and show visitors how Williamsburg residents lived during the colonial era.

At Colonial Williamsburg, you can see the Magazine and Guardhouse near where John drilled with his brother George's volunteer company. You can also tour the Governor's Palace, where swords, pistols, and muskets are on display. And you can visit the milliner where John's sister Betsey secretly met with her beau, Edmund Randolph.

The Colonial Williamsburg Foundation is proud to have worked with Joan Lowery Nixon on the Young Americans series. Staff members met with Mrs. Nixon and identified sources for her research. People at Colonial Williamsburg read each book to make sure it was as accurate as possible, from the way the characters speak, to what they eat, to the clothes they wear. Mrs. Nixon's note at the end of the book tells exactly what we know about John, his family, and his friends.

Another way to learn more about the life of John Nicholas and his family and friends is to experience Williamsburg for yourself. A visit to Colonial Williamsburg is a journey to the past—we invite you to join us on that journey and bring history to life.

Rex M. Ellis
Vice President—Historic Area
The Colonial Williamsburg Foundation

John's Story
1775

More stories in the

YOUNG AMERICANS

Colonial Williamsburg

SERIES BY JOAN LOWERY NIXON

ANN'S STORY: 1747
CAESAR'S STORY: 1759
NANCY'S STORY: 1765
WILL'S STORY: 1771
MARIA'S STORY: 1773

YOUNG AMERICANS

Colonial Williamsburg

John's Story
1775

JOAN LOWERY NIXON

Delacorte Press

Published by
Delacorte Press
an imprint of
Random House Children's Books
a division of Random House, Inc.
1540 Broadway
New York, New York 10036

Text copyright © 2001 by Joan Lowery Nixon and the Colonial Williamsburg Foundation
Back matter copyright © 2001 by the Colonial Williamsburg Foundation
Photographs courtesy of the Colonial Williamsburg Foundation
Produced by 17th Street Productions

Visit us on the Web! www.randomhouse.com/kids
Educators and librarians, for a variety of teaching tools, visit us at
www.randomhouse.com/teachers

Library of Congress Cataloging-in-Publication Data

Nixon, Joan Lowery.
    John's story, 1775 / by Joan Lowery Nixon.
      p. cm. — (Young Americans; 6)
    Summary: In Williamsburg in 1775, as events threaten to plunge the colonies into war
with Britain, eleven-year-old John feels caught between the revolutionary sentiments of his
older brother and his father's insistence on a more temperate and patient course of action.
    ISBN 0-385-32688-2
    1. Williamsburg (Va.)—History—Colonial period, ca. 1600–1775—Juvenile
fiction. [1. Williamsburg (Va.)—History—Colonial period, ca. 1600–1775—
Fiction. 2. Fathers and sons—Fiction. 3. Family life—Fiction. 4. United States—History—
Revolution, 1775–1783—Causes—Fiction.] I. Title.
    PZ7.N65 Jo 2001
    [Fic]—dc21

                                                                              2001042338

The text of this book is set in 12-point Minion.
Book design by Patrice Sheridan
Manufactured in the United States of America
December 2001
10 9 8 7 6 5 4 3 2 1
BVG

Contents

John's Story: 1775   **5**

Author's Note   138

About Williamsburg   144

Childhood in Eighteenth-Century Virginia   154

Revolution in Eighteenth-Century Virginia   161

Recipe for Queen's Cake   166

Prologue

Lori Smith ran ahead of her friends to Molly Otts's booth in Market Square. She leaned on the counter, catching her breath. "Our class just visited the Magazine," she said. "We heard how the British royal marines stole into the Magazine at night and took fifteen half-barrels of gunpowder."

Lori's friends raced to catch up with her. "It was on April 21, 1775," Stewart Dowling added.

Chip Hahn picked up one of the cocked hats for sale at Molly Otts's booth. He planted it firmly on his head, then pretended to rest a rifle against his left shoulder. "Governor Dunmore ordered the marines to take the gunpowder," he said. "I don't like Lord Dunmore, and I don't like his order to steal ammunition from the colonists."

Halim Jordan nodded. "Yeah," he said. "Especially sneaking in while everyone was asleep."

Chip pretended to hold a rifle out for inspection, then shifted it back to his shoulder. "I'm ready to fight for America's independence," he said.

Lori sighed and rolled her eyes, but Mrs. Otts shook her head. " 'Tis plain to see you think the colonists sought a different kind of independence, lads. In 1775 the citizens of Williamsburg were not trying to be free from Great Britain. Most of them thought of themselves as loyal Britons. They just wanted the kind of independence the British colonies in America had had for generations. Parliament made the laws that pertained to the whole empire, and they governed trade, but the colonists wanted their own legislatures to continue to make the laws that governed each colony. They also wanted the right to trial by a jury of their peers in their own colony and to be taxed only by their own elected representatives.

"They felt it was wrong for laws passed by Parliament and King George III in the 1760s and 1770s to take away some of those rights. Even though a war was beginning in 1775, it was seen at that time as a fight to protect their traditional British liberties, their rights."

Keisha Martin asked, "Did all the colonists agree that this was the best thing to do?"

"Some did not agree, and for the majority—well, the way to achieve the colonies' ends, 'twas not a simple matter. Some of Virginia's most respected leaders, such as Robert Carter Nicholas, hoped to reach their goal through reasonable persuasion.

"Others, like his eldest son, George, who was a student at the College of William and Mary, were bent on action to show the Crown that the colonists meant business. Ah, 'tis sure there were many angry words spoken between deliberate, conservative father and impulsive, hotheaded son."

"Whose story is it?" Stewart asked as he moved closer. "I thought you said it would be about George Nicholas's brother John."

Mrs. Otts smiled. "Ah, yes, indeed. My story has to do with George's eleven-year-old brother, John Nicholas. He loved and admired both his father and his eldest brother, so you can imagine how hard it must have been for him to decide where his loyalty lay. On Friday, April 21, 1775, when an early-morning alarm sounded, waking the citizens of Williamsburg . . ."

She stopped speaking and motioned to a nearby bench in the shade. "Let us make ourselves comfortable before I tell you about the events beginning on that early April morning that so frightened young John Nicholas."

Chapter One

John Nicholas awoke groggily to the steady *rat-tat-tat* of drums. "Why is an alarm being sounded?" he asked aloud, even though there was no one but his younger brother, eight-year-old Lewis, to answer him.

Lewis, his blond, tousled head nearly buried under the quilt, simply murmured in his sleep, unaware of questions or answers.

John pushed back the cotton bed hangings and jumped from the high-post bed. Stumbling in the pale morning light and then hopping on one foot as he tried to rub the toe he had stubbed, he threw open the bedchamber door. He staggered into the passageway, his heart racing.

When John heard the front door slam with a firm

thud, he ran to the landing and leaned over the railing. Below him, in the center of the hall, stood his father, Robert Carter Nicholas, wearing his dressing gown and cap, his head bent over a sheet of paper as he read the message on it.

"What is it, Husband?" Mrs. Nicholas asked.

John sucked in his breath as he heard the concern in his mother's voice. He watched her hurry to his father's side, lightly touching his arm for reassurance.

John was well aware that his mother, Anne Nicholas, insisted on proper behavior from all of her children, and eavesdropping on the conversations of others was strongly frowned upon. But at this moment, he didn't worry about rules. The steady drumbeats were frightening, and he needed to know what was taking place that was important enough to alert all the people in Williamsburg.

John saw that he was not alone in his curiosity. He could see Samson, his father's personal body slave, standing just inside the arched doorway to the parlor. Obviously, Samson was listening, too.

As Lewis ran barefoot to his side, John could hear his older sisters, Betsey and Mary, awaken. They called out to each other and to their personal slaves, their voices muted only slightly by the closed bedchamber door.

"Help us dress quickly," John heard Betsey say. "Something is wrong. We must find out what it is."

Girls! John wished they'd be quiet. He rested a hand on Lewis's shoulder and strained forward, hoping he would not miss a word of what his father would tell his mother.

Mr. Nicholas dropped the note to his side and turned to Mrs. Nicholas with an agonized shake of his head. "The action was outrageous!" he exclaimed. "Governor Dunmore— What could the man have been thinking?"

"What has the governor done?" Mrs. Nicholas's voice seemed deliberately low and soft, and John could see that it had a soothing effect on his father. John was not surprised. His short, slender mother had always calmly and efficiently managed her large household, taught and directed her seven children, and supervised the many household slaves. She rarely lost her composure. John gripped the railing eagerly, waiting for his father to answer.

Mr. Nicholas let out such a deep sigh it shook his large frame. Then he answered by reading the message that had been sent to him. " 'A short while ago, between four and five this morning, a company of seamen from the H.M.S. *Magdalen,* which is anchored at Burwell's Landing on the James River, removed fifteen half-barrels of gunpowder from our

7

Public Magazine.' They acted under Governor Dunmore's orders."

John smothered a gasp, clapping a hand over his mouth. Lewis moved closer, pressing against John for comfort, and John gripped his shoulder.

He heard his mother ask with disbelief in her voice, "They stole Virginia's military supplies?"

"Nearly all the powder. They left in a great hurry when they were discovered. Perhaps that is why they did not take the more than three hundred new muskets that were stored in the Magazine."

"What will we do?"

"My concerns are for the present," Mr. Nicholas told her. "You hear the alarm, as does all of Williamsburg. I have been notified that a great many angry men are gathering at Market Square. I fear there will be trouble."

Mrs. Nicholas took a step back, her hands to her face. "George!" she whispered. "Our son George will be there."

Mr. Nicholas scowled. "I fully expect that young man and his rebellious friends to be a part of the mob, ready to cause trouble."

John began to turn, ready to dash to his bedchamber and dress. If action was to be taken at the Magazine, he wanted to be on hand. He was eleven years old, nearly grown—not a child, no matter what his father thought. But he stopped as he heard the firmness that returned to his mother's voice as she defended George.

"Be fair, Husband," Mrs. Nicholas said. "You know they are not trying to cause trouble. Many in Captain James Innes's company are fine young men like George, students at the college. Their independent company of soldiers—"

"Soldiers?" Mr. Nicholas interrupted. "These young men are *playing* soldier, strutting about with no heed for prudence or patience in resolving our differences with the Crown."

John squirmed, wishing he could speak out. He hated it when his father and George disagreed or when his family was divided in any way.

The company to which George belonged was one of many formed to support the local committees responsible for enforcing the embargo on trade with Great Britain. His father knew that. But Robert Carter Nicholas's mind was made up. Negotiations with King George III and Parliament must be handled peacefully. Many of the colonies' leaders, among them Patrick Henry, had formed companies of volunteer soldiers. Mr. Nicholas even approved of the companies. He agreed they were necessary. What he objected to was forceful action that might interfere with reasonable discussions between Great Britain and the colonies.

"Samson!" Mr. Nicholas called.

As Samson quickly stepped forward, Mr. Nicholas told him, "I must dress immediately and leave for Market Square."

Mr. Nicholas turned to Mrs. Nicholas and explained, "There was more to the message than that which I read. I have been called to appeal to the crowd to disband."

Again, John could hear the fear in his mother's voice. "Surely you will not go alone?"

"This summons is from Mayor John Dixon. He will be there. He has also sent for Peyton Randolph."

John knew of Peyton Randolph, Speaker of the House of Burgesses. If the mayor had summoned him, this was sure to be an important task.

As their father turned toward the stairway, Lewis bolted, and John raced back to his bedchamber. He knew that if his father caught sight of him, he'd insist that John remain in safety with his mother, sisters, and brothers. But John had no wish to remain at home—not with militiamen and angry townspeople and all the excitement that might take place. Besides, hadn't his parents said that George might very well have joined the crowd at Market Square? If George was going to be there, then John wanted to be there, too.

John felt a burst of pride as he thought about his brother. But he acknowledged a twinge of envy because George was old enough to help lead a volunteer company and take part in the protest, and he wasn't.

As he tugged on his stockings and buttoned his breeches, John muttered to Lewis, "It's not fair that I'm not yet grown! I want to be able to help. Father treats me as if I were just a child. He won't even teach me how to load and shoot a gun until I'm old enough to accompany him on a hunt. And George laughed when I asked him to let me join his company."

His brown curly hair still uncombed and his coat buttoned askew, John slipped quietly out the front door and ran as fast as he could across Francis Street, past the Magazine, toward Market Square.

The mob that had gathered in the square was even more upset and unruly than John had imagined. People were shouting, some of them pushing as they tried to be heard. Many carried rifles. Had everyone who lived in Williamsburg answered the alarm?

Swept into the middle of the mob, John squeezed

his way through a forest of sharp elbows and knees and a few well-rounded stomachs. He worked his way toward a group of volunteers at one side of the square. "George!" John shouted. "Where are you?"

The noise around him was so great John knew his voice couldn't be heard, but in desperation he shouted again.

Suddenly, he heard a familiar voice and looked through the crowd to see his tall, slender brother, who was standing on a bench waving his gun. Dressed as many of the independent companies were, in a rough brown hunting shirt with a tomahawk stuck in his belt, George was an awesome sight to John.

"To the palace!" George shouted. "We will demand the return of our powder!"

"To the palace!" someone in the crowd shouted, and others excitedly picked up the cry.

John felt a tug on his arm and turned in surprise to see his best friend, eleven-year-old Robert Waller, who was the freckle-faced, red-haired son of Benjamin Waller, lawyer and clerk of the General Court and burgess for James City County.

"I'm going with George!" John yelled at Robert.

"Then I'm going, too!" Robert shouted back.

Heads down, shoulders hunched, John and Robert butted and pushed through the crowd until they reached George. John tugged at George's coat, crying, "We're going to the palace with you! Give us guns!"

For an instant, George could only stare at John. Then his surprise turned to laughter. "I'll not give you guns, lads. You're only children."

John scowled at George. He could feel his face and neck burning. "We are *not* children!" he shouted. "We are—"

George interrupted. "Protecting our colony is a job for men, not young lads like you two. Better get home before your fathers come searching for you."

A few of the men nearby had taken notice and stood watching, smiles on their faces.

John's feelings were hurt. He was embarrassed, and he quickly struck back.

"Father *is* coming," he shouted. "But he'll be looking for *you*, not for me. He told Mother that you'd be here playing soldier."

"He said that, did he?" George's eyes flashed with anger as he jumped down from the bench, and John wished he had kept the remark to himself.

"I'm sorry. I should not have said—" John began, but George's anger had quickly changed to amusement, and he smiled at John, clapping his shoulder. "Never mind, Brother. No harm done. 'Tis not your fault that Father and I do not agree."

John took a deep breath and tried again. "May Robert and I march to the palace with you?"

"Yes, you may march with us, but no weapons. Not yet," George answered. "Wait until you're older to ask for guns."

John grabbed Robert's arm and pulled him into the company of soldiers, working their way to the last straggling line. "We'd make good soldiers, given just half a chance," John complained.

Robert nodded vigorously. "We could quickly learn to fire a gun. How difficult could it be?"

"Not difficult at all," John said. "At least not for us." He looked beyond the militia to his brother, who again was waving his gun and urging the crowd to march to the palace.

The crowd surged from the square toward Palace green but stopped as three men blocked the way.

John recognized the men: plump Peyton Randolph, Speaker of the House of Burgesses and president of the Continental Congress; John's own father, Robert Carter Nicholas, who was a member of the House of Burgesses and treasurer of the Virginia colony; and John Dixon, mayor of Williamsburg.

Peyton Randolph held up a commanding hand, his dark red waistcoat glowing in the bright morning sunlight. "Do not storm the palace in anger," he said.

14

"Impulsive action will benefit nothing and will cause only harm."

Mayor Dixon echoed Mr. Randolph's words as he spoke to the crowd. Some of the men listened, but many continued to grumble angrily among themselves.

"Governor Dunmore had no right to steal our powder!" George called out.

"You are correct, sir!" a voice cried out. "He must return it."

Robert Carter Nicholas stepped forward. "We agree that we must protest what has been done," he said in a calm voice that was strong enough to reach every man in the crowd. "But the position we hold is that it will be more effective to send a delegation to the governor to protest in peace, not in violence."

"Dunmore will not listen to our entreaties, sir," George shot back.

John saw his father take a deep, steadying breath before he answered. "We cannot be positive of this until we try. And it is important not to act in anger, without thought and planning. We must attempt peaceful methods first."

Near John, a man said loudly, "That makes good sense to me." He and two companions left the crowd and began to walk away.

Mr. Randolph and Mayor Dixon added their arguments to those of Mr. Nicholas, and others nodded agreement, stepping aside and leaving the street. Finally, most of the people who had come to protest left, heading toward their homes.

George and his company followed the committee, ready to stand by on the green as they confronted the governor.

John was surprised not only by what had just happened, but by the change in his own feelings from the excitement of confronting the governor to the realization that more could be accomplished by a peaceful discussion. He thought about what his father, Mr. Randolph, and Mayor Dixon had said to calm and convince the crowd. He had been moved by their arguments and the good sense behind them, and he was very proud of his father.

But he was proud of George, too. George was willing to fight for the Crown's recognition of Virginia's rights, and that took courage.

Robert spoke up, breaking into John's thoughts. "Do you think Governor Dunmore will listen to your father?"

"I don't know," John said. "I can only hope he will. My father believes that if we are patient and conduct ourselves as good and responsible citizens, King George and Parliament will come to value cooperation with the colonies."

Robert nodded. "My father believes the same," he said.

"Perhaps they are right," John answered, "but if Father is right, then George and his friends are wrong. And men like Patrick Henry, who spoke out for liberty at the Virginia Convention, are wrong, too."

Who is right and who is wrong? John's head hurt as he thought about the question. It was too hard to decide.

"Did you hear about the speech Patrick Henry gave at the convention in Richmond last month?" John asked. "George reminded Father that Mr. Henry was not speaking about peace and reconciliation when he said there is no longer any room for hope and that we must fight."

"I heard," Robert said. "My father told me that Mr. Henry also raised his arms to the heavens and cried, 'Give me liberty or give me death.' "

Death. John wondered if Mr. Henry would really choose so easily to die. Solemnly, he asked Robert, "Have you ever seen a dead man?"

"No," Robert answered. "Have you?"

"No." John tried to imagine believing in something so much he would be willing to give his life for it, but he couldn't. As he looked around, he saw that his father was busy speaking with the mayor, and the crowd had thinned to only a few stragglers. "We'd better get home before our mothers miss us," John said. "I'll come by your house this afternoon."

Robert grinned. "I'll beat you again at mumblety-peg," he said. He turned and ran toward his home, which was at the far end of Francis Street.

John, with a shorter way to go, walked more slowly. There was much to think about. The possibility of fighting for liberty with muskets and swords was exciting enough to make his heart beat faster. If it came to a fight, he'd prove that he was not too young to join in—but liberty or death! No! He shuddered. Not death.

He prayed that his father's peaceful approach would be the right one.

Chapter Two

Later that Friday morning, John came to the breakfast table with his clothes tidied, his face washed, and his hair neatly combed. He slipped quietly into his chair, bowing his head as his father led the family in morning prayers.

Mrs. Nicholas silently filled each plate with several slices of bacon and two Indian flapjacks fresh from the griddle. Titus, one of their many slaves, stood nearby so he could assist if needed. Then Mr. Nicholas related to Mrs. Nicholas the events that had taken place at Palace green.

As he spoke of his efforts to calm the mob, which had been bent on violence, she murmured approval. But as soon as she had the chance, Mrs. Nicholas put down her fork and asked, "Pray,

Husband, what of our son George? Was he with the crowd?"

Mr. Nicholas frowned. "Yes. He was there, with his volunteer company, and—as I feared—intent on causing trouble."

John, hoping for a fair report about his brother, spoke up heedlessly. "Father, George caused no trouble. He argued with you, but then he did as you asked and stayed with his company to guard you when you approached the governor."

He stopped, clapping a hand over his mouth, as he realized he had given himself away.

John looked quickly at his sisters. After amused glances in John's direction, Betsey and Mary bent their heads demurely, eating with small bites as their mother had taught them. Wilson, who was fourteen and spent most of his time poring over books, stared at John with curiosity. Lewis stopped licking the buttery crumbs from the flapjacks from his fingers and whispered, "Uh-oh!"

But Mr. Nicholas simply nodded. "I saw you in the crowd, John," he said. "I hope you learned from the experience that violence achieves nothing, that vulgar displays of shouting and threatening solve nothing."

Mrs. Nicholas turned to Wilson. "Did you go with John?" she asked.

Wilson shook his head as he answered, "No, Mother. I could see no sense in joining the protesters when I had Latin study to do."

Mr. Nicholas nodded. "I am glad to say that Wilson sets an example of industry for which all young men should strive. I would be happy if George concentrated on his studies at William and Mary in the same way." He looked pointedly at John and said, "John, as well."

John wasn't in the mood for a lecture or for hearing more about his father's displeasure with George. Besides, he was eager to know what had happened after the delegation was formed to meet with the governor. Peyton Randolph had reported that the governor's response was "satisfactory," but John wanted to know much more. "Father, pray tell us, did the peaceful delegation to Governor Dunmore succeed?" he asked. "Will the governor order the marines to return our powder?"

Mr. Nicholas's face flushed a deep red. He broke off a piece of flapjack, the cornmeal crumbs falling to his plate, and kept his eyes on them as he answered, "Our delegation explained to Governor Dunmore that the powder belongs to the colony, not to the Crown. We demanded its immediate return, since we've recently heard rumors of slave unrest."

21

John eagerly leaned forward. "Did the governor agree?"

"He said he intended to write to the British ministry that he'd heard the same rumors and had only taken the powder to protect it from the slaves. He promised to return it promptly if it was needed."

"But, Father," John said, "that means he may or may not, so nothing was really settled."

Mr. Nicholas cleared his throat impatiently. "Resolving the situation takes time, John. Both wisdom and patience are needed."

John was surprised. The crowd had been swayed by what Mayor Dixon, Mr. Randolph, and his father had told them. Why hadn't the governor been swayed, too? "Then, in spite of what the people were told, Governor Dunmore's answer was *not* satisfactory," John complained.

"His answer was satisfactory for the moment," Mr. Nicholas muttered. He popped the piece of flapjack into his mouth and slowly chewed it.

John sighed with disappointment and leaned back in his chair. If his father's peaceful ways hadn't been successful, then perhaps George's desired show of force would have been best. *I wish I were old enough to march along with George in James Innes's company,* John thought.

"Let us speak of more pleasant matters," Mrs. Nicholas said in a deliberately cheerful voice. She smiled at Mary. "Daughter, Mr. Pelham reported to me that you have been quite industrious in your practice upon the spinet. Perhaps this afternoon you will play a selection for us."

Mary, who at sixteen was a younger image of her mother, looked pleased. She nodded agreement and took a last sip of coffee.

In the silence that followed, John noticed Betsey's fingers nervously rolling and folding the edges of the napkin that lay bunched in her lap. "Father," Betsey said in a voice so small it could scarcely be heard, "I know that Edmund Randolph has asked your permission to call upon me. Have you given him your decision?"

John saw the flash of quick concern on his mother's face as she quickly said, "Perhaps we should discuss this matter later, Daughter. Did I mention that yesterday I had tea with Sally? Her dear little Courtenay called me Grandmama in the sweetest voice."

Mr. Nicholas leaned forward. His voice booming in contrast to Betsey's soft tones, he said, "Yes, Daughter, Edmund Randolph has requested permission to call upon us. But why should there be any discussion at all? He should know he is not welcome in this household."

Betsey gave a little cry, no louder than a kitten's mew, but Mr. Nicholas didn't seem to notice and continued speaking.

"As you may remember, after the scandal nine years ago in the treasurer's office, when I was appointed treasurer for the colony of Virginia, I was forced to battle the Randolph family in working to separate the treasurership and speakership of the colony." He gave a sharp nod of satisfaction. "And I succeeded."

John was too young to remember this incident, but he'd heard his father speak of it many times before. Mr. Nicholas continued, "That left Peyton Randolph with the speakership alone, and the succession to the post of attorney general for his brother, John Randolph. Unfortunately, during this struggle over who would occupy these powerful government posts, many harsh words were spoken by John Randolph. Peyton Randolph and I have come to terms over the years because we have had to work together in the House of Burgesses, but I share nothing at all with John Randolph. Nothing! That applies to his son, Edmund, as well."

Betsey, without asking to be excused, jumped up from her chair and fled from the room in tears.

John was as confused by this behavior as his father appeared to be. Looking amazed, Mr. Nicholas asked, "What is the matter with Betsey? Why should she become upset because I do not want Edmund Randolph to call upon us?"

"The young man does not wish to call upon you and me, Husband," Mrs. Nicholas answered. "He wishes to call upon Betsey."

"What? Our daughter? Our child?"

"Edmund and Betsey are not children," Mrs. Nicholas explained quietly. "They are both nearly twenty-two years of age." She smiled as she added, "I'm sure you remember they were born on August eleventh—the very same day. When they were young, they were even schoolmates at the school conducted by our parish minister."

Mr. Nicholas scowled. "Betsey is too young to think of courtship and marriage."

"As I mentioned, Betsey will soon be twenty-two. I was barely seventeen when we were wed."

Married? thought John. *Someone wants to marry Betsey?* "That's different," Mr. Nicholas insisted. "I was an intelligent young man who approached the future with good common sense. Edmund is a favored student of that unorthodox gentleman Reverend Samuel Henley, whom I opposed when he applied for the position of minister of Bruton Parish

Church. Therefore I assume that Edmund is no more sensible than his father on religious, political, and personal grounds."

Mrs. Nicholas's eyes sparkled. "Husband, you must not be so quick to judge Edmund. Last year when his cousin, Thomas Jefferson, retired from the practice of law, he thought so highly of Edmund that he turned his clients over to him. And Edmund was appointed clerk to the Committee on Courts and Justice of the House of Burgesses at about that same time. He is a fine, upstanding young man with a good future."

"Edmund, madam, is an impetuous young man and is as much danger to peaceful negotiations with the Crown and Parliament as is our rash son George." Mr. Nicholas carefully laid his napkin beside his plate and pushed back his chair. "I can find no reason to give my permission for Edmund Randolph to call upon our daughter."

As Mr. Nicholas left the room, Mrs. Nicholas jumped up and headed for the stairway—most likely to soothe Betsey, John thought. John couldn't imagine why Edmund Randolph would want to marry silly Betsey. Still, he seemed like a nice enough fellow, and if Thomas Jefferson liked him, he must have some positive qualities. But John himself had no time for girls and their tears. The sooner he finished his lessons, the sooner he'd be free to join Robert for their game of mumblety-peg. He'd been practicing with the special pocketknife George had given him when he turned eleven. The knife had long belonged to George, and his initials were scratched into one side. It was well balanced and flipped easily, quivering as it landed straight up, its sharp point piercing the circles drawn in the dirt. John was sure he could beat Robert this time.

But the game didn't take place. Late that afternoon, Robert ran to meet John halfway down Francis Street. "Did you hear?" he shouted as he came close. "Did you hear that the royal marines from Lieutenant Collins's ship will return tonight to steal what they didn't take the first time?"

John stopped short. "The rest of the gunpowder and the muskets?"

"Yes!"

"At the governor's orders?"

"I don't know," Robert admitted. "Mrs. Gooseley heard it from Mistress Rathell, the milliner. Mistress Rathell heard the news when she was at Mr. Greenhow's store. I heard Mrs. Goosley tell my mother."

John thought quickly. "Captain James Innes,

William Finnie, and my brother George will be there to defend the Magazine. We should be there, too, so that we might lend a hand."

"George said he will not give us guns."

"Who knows what will happen if the royal marines from the H.M.S. *Magdalen* and the Williamsburg volunteers do battle against each other?" John asked. He could feel his heart quicken, and he took a deep breath. With great seriousness, he said, "Robert, we are old enough to fight if we are needed."

Robert sighed. "Unless our parents find out."

For an instant, John felt a twinge of guilt. He had always been an obedient son. But life had suddenly changed. The Magazine had been attacked. From what Robert had heard, it would be attacked again. How could the people of Williamsburg allow this to happen?

"We can't let the royal marines carry off the rest of our supplies," John said firmly.

"No, we can't," Robert echoed.

"We must be on hand to defend Virginia."

"Against the royal marines."

"And Governor Dunmore." Lowering his voice and carefully glancing around to see if he was being overheard, John added, "Meet me across the street from my house after supper."

"I'll be there," Robert said.

John hadn't realized how difficult it would be to choke down every mouthful of sliced meat and bread at supper. With his mind on what might take place at the Magazine in a short while, he wasn't the least bit hungry. But if he didn't eat, his mother would feel his forehead, suspecting fever, and send him off to bed. His mother never missed a thing.

Mr. Nicholas ate silently, and John wondered if he had heard the rumors, too. Would his father again attempt to quiet those who gathered to resist the British marines? What if the marines appeared, ready once again to carry out the governor's orders? What would his father do then?

"John," Mrs. Nicholas said.

Startled, John jumped, sloshing milk from his glass onto the tablecloth. As he put down his glass, steadying it with both hands, his elbow brushed the edge of his plate, and his fork clattered to the floor. "Y-yes, Mother?" he managed to ask. He could feel his face burn with embarrassment.

"Are you not well?" she asked. "I have noticed that you seem to have trouble eating, and your cheeks are flushed. Come here, child."

"I am well, Mother. I am just not hungry," John

said, but he obediently walked to her side and bent to allow her to rest her palm against his forehead.

The tips of her fingers felt cool against his skin, so he was not surprised when she told him, "I think it best that you leave the table and go to bed. You do not seem feverish, so perhaps a good night's sleep will be all that you need."

"Yes, Mother," John answered, but as he climbed the stairs, he wondered what he was going to do. Surely his mother would come in to feel his head again before she went to her own bedchamber, but that might be much later, and Robert would be expecting him.

It was not until Lewis came into the bedchamber shortly after supper that John came up with an idea. He told Lewis what Robert had heard about the marines returning and confided, "I'm going to meet Robert and go to the Magazine. We're going to help defend the rest of our supplies."

Lewis's eyes widened. "Will Father allow you to go?"

John shrugged. "I see no need to ask his permission."

"But—"

"He didn't tell me I couldn't. It's the same thing."

Lewis's eyes sparkled. "Mother will find out when she discovers you are not in bed."

John took Lewis's arms and pulled him close.

"That's where you can help out," he said. "I want you to sleep on my side of the bed. Lie on your side away from the doorway and pull the quilt over most of your face. In the candlelight, Mother will think you are me."

Lewis looked skeptical. "She will see that my side of the bed is empty."

"Not if we stuff it with pillows."

At first Lewis grinned with delight, but he soon looked up at John with a serious expression. "I want to defend the Magazine, too," he said.

"You can't," John answered, "or our plan won't work."

Lewis scowled, his lower lip curling out. "It's not *our* plan. It's *your* plan. Besides, if you get into trouble, then so will I."

John thought a moment. He remembered the wistful look on Lewis's face when he saw George give John his pocketknife. "I don't want to be unfair," John said. "Maybe I should give you something to make it come out even."

Lewis's eyes narrowed. "Give me *what* something?"

"The ownership of my pocketknife for the period of a week."

"Really?" Lewis smiled. "Do you mean that I could carry it in my pocket and you couldn't touch it?"

John nodded. "For an entire week."

31

"Done," Lewis said. He held out his right hand, palm up. When John placed the pocketknife in it, Lewis gripped it tightly.

A short time later, Lewis lay in John's place in bed, and pillows were lumped under the quilt where Lewis would normally sleep. Satisfied, John slipped down the stairs and out the back door. He ran through the darkness to find Robert squirming with impatience.

"What took you so long?" Robert complained.

"I'll tell you later," John said. He could see the torches carried by men who were gathering at the other side of the Magazine. "Hurry!" he exclaimed. "We don't want to miss a thing!"

As John and Robert ran to join the crowd, they saw George and his friend William Finnie with their volunteer company. Both were addressing the people who had come to the Magazine.

"The governor had no right to steal our gunpowder!" William called out.

"Governor Dunmore is a thief!" someone in the crowd shouted, and others loudly agreed.

George cried, "We will not let this deliberate action against us happen again! We vow to take up arms against the marines if they return to steal more of our ammunition!"

Again, men in the crowd shouted their support,

and John, his heart thumping with excitement, shouted, too.

"We'll fight!" he yelled, jumping up and down.

"We'll fight!" Robert echoed.

As others ran to join the crowd and William and George continued to stir up emotions against Governor Dunmore, John kept peering through the darkness toward the south—the direction from which the royal marines would come.

He'd shout a warning the very moment he spied their torches and heard their marching feet.

John clutched Robert's arm. "When the marines arrive, we are going to fight!" he shouted through the din.

His heart gave a quick skip, and he gulped hard as he repeated in a whisper to himself, "We are actually going to fight!"

Chapter Three

Contrary to the rumors that had swept through Williamsburg, the royal marines did not come back to the Magazine. Eventually, the men who had gathered to protect the Magazine drifted away, returning to their homes. Exhausted and disappointed that nothing exciting had happened, John climbed into bed next to Lewis and immediately fell asleep.

He was still sleeping long after the sun rose the next morning. In his dream, he heard loud voices in argument.

"Go away," he mumbled. He tried to pull the pillow over his head, but the shouting grew louder, and he began to recognize the voices.

"Father?" he asked aloud as he struggled to sit up in bed. "George? Lewis?"

But Lewis was no longer in the room, and the door had been left ajar.

John slid out of bed, pulled on his breeches, and ran into the passage. Now he could hear the argument clearly, since his father and George stood in the hall directly below the landing.

"Listen to me, George! Pay close attention! I wish to read what our governor said about you," Mr. Nicholas commanded.

"Father, you must know that I am not the least bit interested in what Dunmore has to say," George answered.

"You had better be interested. It concerns you personally," Mr. Nicholas retorted, and John could imagine the angry look on his father's face.

There was a pause. Then George said, "I fail to see why Dunmore has any interest in me."

"Unfortunately, he has," Mr. Nicholas said, "as you will discover when you hear the message that was sent to me by Dr. William Pasteur, who heard these words from Governor Dunmore himself."

John could hear the sneer in George's voice as he replied, "I thought you said the message was from the governor. He cannot speak for himself?"

Mr. Nicholas ignored the remark and read aloud, " 'Governor Dunmore swore that if a grain of powder was burnt at Captain Foy or Lieutenant Collins, or—' "

"Dunmore does not express himself clearly. Does he mean if they are shot at?" George laughed.

"You know what he means," Mr. Nicholas snapped. "Pray allow me to continue. '. . . If any injury or insult is offered to himself or either of them, he will arm the slaves, declare their freedom, and reduce the city of Williamsburg to ashes. His Excellency then asked me to convey his message to the Speaker of the House of Burgesses and to other gentlemen of the town who—' "

"*Influential* gentlemen, I presume, which includes you, Father."

"Pray do not interrupt, George. Dr. Pasteur goes on to write, 'There is not an hour to spare.' Then he adds the governor's admonition that if William Finnie and George Nicholas continue to go at large, what he has said will, from some misconduct of theirs, be carried into execution."

Execution! thought John. Before he could stop himself, John ran down the stairs and shouted, "You must not be executed, George! You must stop these actions!" But George only chuckled, and soon his laughter turned into a roar. When he was finally able to talk, he asked, "The governor will burn Williamsburg because of Finnie and me? I assure you, Father and Brother, it will not happen."

Mr. Nicholas's voice was stern. "Perhaps that

threat was exaggerated by Governor Dunmore's anger, but I fear that in his fury, he could very well carry out his threat to free and arm slaves who agree to join the British. He vows that if he is antagonized by you and William, he will destroy Williamsburg and depopulate the entire colony."

George laughed again. "Dunmore is a fool to make such ill-considered threats. Do you think that Patrick Henry and his troops or Hugh Mercer and his many volunteers will allow Dunmore to carry them out?"

Mr. Nicholas let out a groan, then asked, "George, can you not realize what might happen if our slaves are freed and armed?"

"Our slaves would never leave us," interrupted John. But George and Mr. Nicholas went on speaking as if he weren't even there.

"Father, that is an idle threat. It means nothing," George answered. "You are allowing the governor to frighten you."

"I am not frightened. I am being realistic."

"Then be realistic enough to admit that the peaceful, rational approach you have adopted has gained nothing for the people of Virginia."

John cowered as his father sputtered with anger. Mr. Nicholas roared, "Our governor has called for your arrest. How much will *you* gain for our Virginia colonists while you reside in a dark and stinking cell in the Public Gaol?"

John could see the glint in George's eye as he said, "Dunmore will have to catch me first."

The argument continued, but John didn't stay to listen. He slowly walked back to his bedchamber, shaken by the idea of slaves' being freed and armed. He had heard his father say not many months before that there were as many slaves as there were colonists in Williamsburg. Would Samson and Titus accept the governor's offer? Samson had been with the Nicholas family for years, and Titus had been purchased from the estate of Virginia's late Governor Botetourt. Both slaves were young, strong, and healthy.

If they were armed, what would they do?

John shuddered. He was frightened, and he needed answers to his questions.

Suddenly, Mrs. Nicholas appeared in the doorway of John's bedchamber. She hurried to his side, clapping the palm of her right hand against his forehead. "Such a frown, dear son," she said. "At least you do not have a fever. Are you still feeling ill? Do you have any pain?"

"I am well, Mother," John answered. He looked up into his mother's worried face and tried to smile.

She studied him for only a moment, then said, "I believe you witnessed the argument between your father and brother. Did what they say cause you worry?"

"Yes, Mother," John said. There was no point in trying to deceive his mother. Sooner or later, she learned everything there was to know about what her children were thinking or doing. He sighed and asked, "Will George be arrested and confined to the Public Gaol?"

"I don't think so," Mrs. Nicholas answered. "The governor spoke quickly, in anger. I pray that he has changed his order already." She sat next to John and put an arm around his shoulders. "Do not worry, dear."

But there was more for John to be concerned about. "Mother," he asked, "what will we do if the governor sets the slaves free and arms them?"

He felt her stiffen for just an instant, but soon she patted his shoulder, smoothed back his hair, and kissed his forehead. "My dear son," she said, "our slaves will not leave us. The governor cannot order them to do so. As for his threats—do not worry about matters of state. Your father will see to our welfare, as he has always done."

John almost groaned aloud. His mother had spoken to him as if he were a small child afraid of dark shadows behind the candlelight. "I am old enough to understand what is taking place, Mother," he said.

"Of course you are, John," she told him. But

instead of answering his question, she stood and smiled, lightly patting his cheek. "You've slept late, dear, but you're up now and feeling well, so dress quickly and join the family for breakfast."

As soon as his mother had left the bedchamber, John hurried to wash his face in the basin in his chamber and finish dressing. He should have known better than to question his mother. It was his father who would be able to give him the answers he wanted. He would try his best to talk to his father before the family meal.

But when John raced down the stairs, his father had already entered the dining room. Two of their household slaves, Betty and her daughter, Diana, were in the adjoining passage. John certainly couldn't ask about a slave rebellion with them nearby, so he edged up to his father and quietly asked, "Sir, may I talk to you privately after breakfast?"

Mr. Nicholas looked down at John with a stern expression. "Do you wish to explain why you were at the Magazine last night?"

John gulped and could feel himself blushing. "No, Father. I mean, yes, Father, I was there. But I wish to speak with you about something else."

"There is a meeting I must attend immediately after breakfast."

"But what I have to ask is important, sir."

"I'm sure it is. And it's important to me to remind

you that you must not attempt to imitate your brother George. How much better if you were to spend your time at study, like your brother Wilson. Do you understand?"

"Yes, Father," John whispered. From the corner of his eyes, he saw Betty and Diana leave their posts. "Father—about the governor freeing and arming the slaves," he asked in a low voice. "What will happen to the people of Williamsburg? Will we all be killed? Will we—"

Mr. Nicholas clamped his hands on John's shoulders. "Son, use your energies for study and self-improvement, not for needless worry about matters beyond your years."

Even though Mr. Nicholas tried to appear calm, John could see his own concern mirrored in his father's eyes. He knew his father was worried, too, about the governor's threats. "Sir," he insisted, "I am not a child. I know what the governor threatened, and I need to know more. I have questions."

Mr. Nicholas slowly shook his head. "John, there are many responsible gentlemen in Williamsburg who can reason with Governor Dunmore. And in spite of the notions of some hotheaded young men like your brother George whose impulsive actions are dangerous to the cause, reason and discussion are our best weapons, not guns."

41

"But, Father—"

Betsey and Mary came into the room, followed by Mrs. Nicholas, and John had no choice but to take his place at the table. Wilson walked in reading, closing his book just before he reached the table. As the family was about to be seated, Lewis rushed to the table, skidding to a stop and nearly toppling his chair.

After pausing for a disapproving look at Lewis, Mr. Nicholas bowed his head and asked a blessing on the food and on their family.

John couldn't keep his mind on his father's long prayer. He was beginning to believe that he and George were the only ones in the family who cared about the future of Virginia. Wilson had no interest in anything but his studies, and Lewis was too young to understand what the fight for liberty was all about. As for Betsey and Mary and even his married sister, Sally—they were only girls, so little could be expected from them.

As soon as breakfast had been eaten, John made himself scarce. Hoping that his mother wouldn't see him and demand an account of what he was up to, John left the house by the back way. He was off to find Robert and tell him about the governor's threats. He badly needed to talk to someone about what was happening. Robert wouldn't have the answers, but at least he would listen and share his own worries.

The air glistened with sunlight, carrying the sharp, clean fragrance of mint from the herb garden as John neared the outdoor kitchen. He suddenly stopped, frozen in shock, as he heard Samson say, "Me? I could fight on the side of the British. That is, if the gov'nor mean what he say and give me my freedom."

John leaned against the brick wall for support. Samson would leave their family and fight *against* George? And Father? In spite of the sun's warmth, John shivered.

He heard Titus speak up. "Sometimes I tell myself, 'Titus, one day you travel west as a freed man.' Now maybe that someday has come round."

"You all just talk," Betty snapped. "Travelin' west. Fightin' with the British soldiers. Huh! The gov'nor made a big threat just to scare people. He won't do nothin' 'bout it. Wait and see."

Titus chuckled. "Well, if he does, Betty, where you goin'? What you plannin' to do?"

There was a long pause before Betty answered. John could hear the fear in her voice. "Where you think I go? I stay right here, where my child and me will be safe. How you think I be able to feed the two of us out on the road someplace?"

Betty's voice dropped. "Besides, Mistress Nicholas always been good to us."

43

Surprise raised Samson's voice. "Don't you want to be free, woman?"

"I must take care of my child," Betty answered. "You tell me how I do that when we free."

John pushed away from the support of the wall. He ran from the garden and from the argument. He didn't want to think about what he had just overheard. He felt sick to his stomach. Farther down Francis Street, out of sight of his home, John flopped to the grass and pressed his hands against his stomach, trying to push the nausea away.

At the back of John's mind grew a nagging question. If liberty meant so much to the Virginians that they were willing to risk their lives for it, then why wouldn't it mean just as much—perhaps even more—to slaves?

"There you are," Robert suddenly said. He dropped down on the grass next to John. "Why are you just sitting here?"

"I had to think," John said.

Robert grinned and elbowed John. "That shouldn't take long," he teased.

John didn't smile. "I've got something important to tell you," he said. He relayed the message his father had received from Dr. Pasteur. But John didn't tell Robert about his father's argument with George or about the slaves' conversation. He would keep this information to himself for a while. It was still very troubling, and there was much to think about.

Robert frowned. "Do you think the governor will really do as he threatened?"

"I don't know," John said. "I tried to talk about it with my father, but he was too busy."

Beside him, Robert shuddered. His voice dropped to a whisper. "During the last few months, I have heard my father speak of a possible uprising among the slaves. Some of his friends were worried about it, too. Then, when the marines stole the powder from the Magazine, my father claimed that Governor Dunmore used the rumors of a slave uprising as an excuse for ordering them to do so."

John looked at Robert in surprise. "Does your father talk to you about what is taking place in the colony?"

Robert squirmed a moment, then met John's gaze. "He talks to my grown brothers, John and Benjamin, not to me. He thinks I am too young to know or care, but sometimes I listen to what they say."

John hugged his arms to his chest as a chill ran up and down his back. "We are not too young to be shot at, Robert," he said. "From what I have heard today, that is very likely to happen!"

Chapter Four

"I don't like to think about being shot," Robert said, his voice trembling. "Let's talk about something else." He scrambled to his feet and shoved his right hand into the pocket of his jacket, pulling out two copper halfpence. "This will buy us each a sugar twist at Mr. Greenhow's store." He held out a hand to John, who grabbed it and jumped to his feet.

"Race you to Duke of Gloucester!" John shouted. He didn't wish to think about the terrible things that might happen, either.

He dashed up Botetourt Street to Duke of Gloucester Street. On the way, he narrowly avoided two men, who jumped aside, and startled a woman, who dropped her empty market basket. Arriving at the corner just steps ahead of Robert, John yelled, "First!"

" 'Twas a tie!" Robert shouted back.

"Boys are such ruffians!" a familiar voice said.

John turned in surprise to see his sister Mary. "We were just racing," he explained.

"I know what you were doing," she said, but she didn't look at John. As she spoke, she kept glancing across the street. "You were frightening passersby and making a great to-do."

John tried to see what Mary was seeing. "What are you looking at?" he asked.

"Nothing. Never mind," she said quickly. She turned and began adjusting the bow that tied her hat under her chin.

But John kept his gaze on the shop Mary had been watching. "Are you bound for the milliner?" he asked.

"Milliner?" Mary gave a start. "No. I am not in need of a new bonnet."

"Then what—?"

At that moment, the door to the milliner's shop opened and John saw his sister Betsey step out. As she came down the steps, a gentleman who had been examining the window display at the silversmith's shop next door stepped to her side. To John's surprise, he saw that it was Edmund Randolph.

Mary gripped John's arm and tried to turn him away from the street and toward her. "I pity our poor milliner, Mistress Rathell," Mary chattered. "Last year, the Continental Congress adopted an agreement forbidding trade with Great Britain, so Mistress Rathell will not be able to get her goods to sell. She has spoken of closing her business and returning to England."

John stopped trying to pull away from Mary and let her turn him away from Betsey and Edmund. He had seen Betsey simpering up at Edmund, and he'd seen the pleased look on Edmund's face. He knew that Betsey—probably with Mary's help—had found a way to be with Edmund in spite of their father's refusal to allow him to come to call.

"How good of Betsey to visit Mistress Rathell in order to discuss the banning of imports and exports," he said, trying to look serious. "And how fine of Edmund Randolph to come and lend *his* voice to the argument."

Mary stepped close and thrust her face into his own. "Listen to me, John Nicholas. Do not say one word about this to Mother or Father," she warned.

John shrugged and tried to look wide-eyed and innocent. "About what?" he asked. "About Betsey becoming interested in agreements to cease trade?"

Mary stamped a foot. "Stop that, John! You can be so aggravating!" she complained.

John laughed. He liked his older sisters in spite of

the fact that they were girls and did silly girl things. And he liked Edmund Randolph. "I am the last person Mother and Father would question about Betsey's comings and goings," he said. "I never know what my sisters are up to."

Betsey fumbled in the pocket of her skirt and brought out a quarter of a Spanish two-real piece. "You are a good boy, John," she said. "You and Robert run down to Mr. Greenhow's store and buy yourselves a sugar treat."

"Mary . . ." John began to give back the coin, but then he decided that two treats were even better than one. "Uh—I thank you," he added.

John and Robert continued down Duke of Gloucester Street through groups of people who strolled, shopped, or lingered to talk.

Along the way, they heard snatches of conversation about the governor's threats. By this time, it seemed to John that everyone in Williamsburg had heard the contents of Dr. Pasteur's message, since the same message had been sent to a number of officials in Williamsburg.

"I, for one, have decided to return to England and safety," a portly gentleman told others who had gathered to talk across from the post office.

"You may have the right idea," one of his companions put in. "Can you imagine what might happen if the slaves are armed?"

A tall, thin gentleman raised a hand. "We must not act in haste," he said. "In order to receive arms, slaves must decide to join Dunmore, run away from their masters, and agree to fight against Virginians. How many do you think will do such a thing?"

How many? John didn't want to know the answer. He didn't want to think about it. He broke into a run, Robert right behind him.

But as they reached Mr. Greenhow's store, a woman near the steps shivered, drawing her shawl close around her. "I fear we will all be killed," she said to her companions. "We have little powder left in the Magazine with which to defend ourselves."

"Which I fear was Governor Dunmore's plan," another woman snapped.

"He is our governor. He should protect us," someone complained.

The first woman shook her head angrily. "Our governor does not want to protect us. He only wants us to agree to whatever Parliament and King George demand of us."

John met Robert's eyes. He wondered if he looked as frightened as Robert did. He certainly didn't want to hear one more word about slave uprisings.

Dashing up the steps side by side, John and Robert laid their coins on Mr. Greenhow's counter. They waited impatiently until it was their turn to be waited on by Mr. Greenhow. Around them, other shoppers were discussing the governor's threats—some in hushed, frightened tones. But one woman spoke loudly and angrily.

"If we are killed in our beds, the blame will lie squarely on Governor Dunmore!" Mrs. Gooseley exclaimed, her chins wobbling in indignation.

A lump of nausea rose in John's throat, and he leaned against the counter for support. Turning to Robert, he said, "I don't feel like eating anything right now."

"Neither do I," Robert agreed, his face pale.

They scooped up their coins from the counter and ran from the store.

Later, as John entered the back door of his house, he surprised Samson and Titus in conversation. Both slaves immediately stopped speaking and stepped apart when they saw him, but from the wary expressions on their faces, John was certain they had again been discussing what the governor had said.

John slowly walked up the stairs to the privacy of his bedchamber, trying to understand what the slaves might feel, but he couldn't. Samson and Titus and the other Nicholas slaves were treated well, he knew. His mother nursed them through their illnesses, they were often given meat and molasses to go with their hominy, and all had sturdy, warm clothing to wear.

They were kindly treated. His father and mother expected their household to run smoothly and efficiently but were rarely harsh with their slaves. What reason would they have to turn against their masters?

What more could they possibly want?

John shrugged, uncomfortable with the questions. He pushed them aside, not wishing to think about them or the answers they might have.

He wished he could talk to his father, but he knew his father was not at home. He was rarely home because of the positions he held: treasurer of the Virginia colony and burgess of James City County, delegate to the Virginia convention, chairman of the James City County Committee, and member of the Williamsburg Committee. Of course, John felt proud of all that his father was doing, but he also wished with all his heart that his father had enough time left to spend with him. John badly needed answers to his questions.

John's lessons at the college's grammar school began again on Monday. There had been no further word or action on the part of Governor Dunmore. Neither George nor William had been arrested, and for the most part, people in town no longer worried aloud about the possible arming of slaves. As John practiced adding and subtracting figures in his copybook or squeezed his forehead into wrinkles trying to decline nouns in Latin, he was immensely grateful that life had returned to normal.

However, at the end of the week, on Thursday, April 27, the terrifying news about the April 19 battles at Lexington and Concord in Massachusetts reached Williamsburg. John saw that he was not the only one who was frightened by the reports.

"Will Williamsburg be attacked next?" people asked one another.

John ran to the volunteers' encampment and was almost out of breath as he reached his brother. "George! The British army will attack us, too, will it not?" he managed to ask.

George didn't try to reassure John. He scowled and answered, "How can any of us know what will happen? The king and Parliament have shown no desire to work out problems with the colonies, as Father hoped they would. Instead, they seem to have decided to use deadly force in an effort to keep all the colonies in line."

"Wh-what will happen to us?" John asked.

George sighed and for the first time seemed to notice John's fear. He put his hands on John's shoulders and looked into his eyes. "You are old enough to be told the truth," he said.

John gulped and tried to stand a little taller, waiting for what George would say. He hoped his brother could not feel the trembling that ran up and down his spine.

"No matter what Father or anyone else says, the time for reasoning with the king and with Parliament has passed," George continued. "The colonies will have to stand together, to share our strengths, to fight to preserve our liberties."

John tried to speak, but he had to clear his throat and start over. "Are you saying that the British army will attack us here in Williamsburg?"

He was surprised to see George smile. "We have to be ready for any eventuality," George said.

"You and James and William and your volunteer companies?" John asked.

"And more," George answered.

"Who?" John persisted.

"You will find out soon enough," George said. "All you have to know for now is that there is nothing for you to fear." He turned John in the direction of the College of William and Mary and gave him both a pat and a push. "Run along, little brother. Shouldn't you be at your studies?"

John stumbled forward a few steps, then turned. He would have liked to retort, "And shouldn't you, too?" But he took a good look at George, who stood tall, arms akimbo, again dressed in the rugged hunting shirt worn by many of the volunteers, and John felt a rush of pride.

George and his friends would see that Williamsburg was well defended. John was certain of it.

And he was even more certain that if it came to fighting the British army or marines, he, John, was going to take part.

It came as no surprise to John the next day when Hugh Mercer, commander of the volunteer company in Fredericksburg, sent out a call for men to march on Williamsburg to protect it.

"Are they mad!" Mr. Nicholas thundered as he read aloud the message that had been delivered.

"Try to remain calm, Husband," Mrs. Nicholas said softly as she rested a hand on his arm.

"Calm? Who can remain calm?" he exclaimed. He slapped the rolled paper against the palm of his left hand. "Mercer expects at least six hundred men to join him to march on Williamsburg! That's all Dunmore needs to provoke him! Armed militia bent on action! Rioting in the streets!"

Mrs. Nicholas sighed and tugged at Mr. Nicholas's arm. "At least be seated," she murmured. "Your face is deeply flushed. Becoming this upset could do you ill."

Pulling away, Mr. Nicholas shouted, "I have no time to be seated! I must send an appeal to Hugh

Mercer in Fredericksburg. His army of volunteers must be stopped!" He paused, thinking a moment before he said, "If our delegates to the Continental Congress have not already left for Philadelphia, they should also appeal to Mercer to keep his men quiet. Where's Samson?"

Samson immediately appeared in the doorway. "Here I am, Master Nicholas," he answered.

"Samson, in a few minutes I'll need you to deliver some letters for me," Mr. Nicholas said.

John watched his father stomp off to the desk where he kept his writing paper, inkwell, quills, and sealing wax.

So this is what George meant, John thought. *He promised me that Williamsburg would be protected. How could he know that Father would think the militia harmful and would try to send them away?*

John silently slipped from the room and ran out of the house. He had a message to deliver, too. He would have to inform George of the action Father was taking.

Chapter Five

George Nicholas and Captain Innes listened intently as John breathlessly related all that he had heard. James slowly shook his head, but George said, "Father, Peyton Randolph, and their friends who hope for reconciliation are fighting a losing battle. Their arguments may succeed in holding back Hugh Mercer's volunteers, but not for long. We will soon be close to a confrontation."

"In Williamsburg?" John whispered, his heart beating rapidly.

"Throughout the colonies," George answered.

John wished his brother had spoken directly about Williamsburg, but before he could ask again, George smiled at John and added, "Thank you for informing us, John. It was a wise thing to do."

John knew it would do no good to question George about information he wanted to keep secret. "I will tell you anything I think you should know," he said.

Solemnly, both George and James shook John's hand, and he left their encampment with pride overriding his fear. Even though he might be too young to fight, he was not too young to help his brother and the volunteers.

Neatly dressed in coat, waistcoat, and linen breeches, George joined the family for supper that evening. Although Mr. Nicholas greeted him formally, Mrs. Nicholas clung to her son's arm, smiling.

"I begged George to join us," she said to her husband. "Lately, he has been so busy we rarely see him."

As she reached her place at the head of the table, George waited for her to be seated before taking his usual place on her right.

As soon as Mr. Nicholas's long blessing had ended, George smiled at Mary and Betsey, who sat directly across the table. "Betsey," he said with a mischievous look in his eyes, "I was asked to tell you that tomorrow afternoon at four Mistress Rathell might have the ribbons you wish for your new straw hat."

Betsey, blushing furiously, tried to suppress a smile. Mary threw John a cautious look, which turned into a warning scowl as he grinned at her.

John knew what George had meant. If George approved of Edmund cnough to carry his secret messages to Betsey, then John approved of Edmund, too. He wasn't about to give away the secret.

But Mr. Nicholas hesitated, the serving fork for the cold sliced chicken in his hand. "Is it not curious, George, that you should be asked to deliver a message from a milliner?" he asked.

Mary interrupted, speaking rapidly. "Father, let us speak of Mistress Rathell. Have you heard that she cannot receive goods from England because of the import and export bans, so she has made it known she will most likely return to England?" When Mr. Nicholas didn't respond, Mary added, "I think she is frightened by the news from Massachusetts as well."

"There is no reason to be frightened," Mr. Nicholas answered. "The colonists' demands are within reason. We must give King George time to consider them."

"Father, the king has had more than enough time." George began to rise from his chair, but Mrs. Nicholas swiftly pulled him down.

Mr. Nicholas leaned toward his son. "George, you must understand that the problem lies not with our king and members of Parliament, but with corrupt ministers who have influenced them for their own selfish gain. Surely the king will come to realize the truth."

"The king will not listen to *us*!"

"Of course he will listen. We must be patient."

George jumped to his feet, pushing back his chair with such force that it toppled with a crash. As Titus ran to set it upright, George shouted, "Father, *you* are the one who must face the truth. During the past few months, we have received news of troop movement in Great Britain, and governors throughout the colonies have been given orders to seize the colonists' ammunition. You have seen what befell the Massachusetts colonists at Lexington and Concord! And recently the governors have been instructed to prevent the second session of Congress. Can you not see that Dunmore's raid on our Magazine was a sign that the colonies are about to be invaded?"

Mary spoke up. "I heard that Lady Dunmore and her children left the palace to stay on the H.M.S. *Fowey,* anchored at Yorktown. Is this true, George?"

Mr. Nicholas answered before George could, and his face showed his surprise and displeasure that Mary had questioned her brother instead of her father. "Lady Dunmore has been concerned about possible danger caused by rebellious youth who act without wisdom or caution," he answered. "Why, two gentlemen of our acquaintance here in town have sent their wives and children into the country for the same reason."

George scowled as he said, "Or perhaps our governor's lady is in a position to know more about Great Britain's plans for the colonies than we do."

Mary gasped. "Do you mean we *will* be invaded?" she whispered.

"Nonsense!" Mr. Nicholas bellowed. "Lady Dunmore was merely concerned about Hugh Mercer and his harebrained scheme to march his volunteers on Williamsburg." He leaned forward and said pointedly to George, "Since you are here with us instead of mustering your volunteers at this moment to join Mercer's forces, you no doubt know that Peyton Randolph, George Washington, Edmund Pendleton, and Richard Henry Lee were among those who sent appeals to Mercer and his company to disband. Although they spent nearly all day debating the appeals, I received word they finally disbanded a short time ago and returned to their homes. It is over."

"I beg to differ with you, Father," George said. "It is not over yet. There are others who—"

"If you are speaking of another irrational hothead, that Patrick Henry, who has his troops quartered in Hanover County and who intended to join Mercer—"

"It is not just Virginia that is preparing," George interrupted, his voice dropping in the silenced room. "The colonies will join together in demanding their liberties."

"But if we are patient—" Mr. Nicholas began again.

George pushed back his chair and rose. With a bow to Mrs. Nicholas, he said, "Pray excuse me, Mother." He gave a short, clipped bow to Mr. Nicholas, then strode from the room, leaving his food untouched.

Although John finished the meal in silence, as did the other members of his family, occasionally he raised his eyes to study his father. Mr. Nicholas's face sagged with exhaustion, and the shadows under his eyes were gray.

They both make good arguments, thought John. *But how can they both be right?*

Oh, Father, John thought, *why can you not see what is taking place?*

But John knew that his father and his opinions always had been highly respected in the community. Perhaps this time, too, he was right, and George and his friends were wrong. At the moment, John's feelings were torn between his father and brother. He didn't know what to believe.

On Sunday, April 30, at two in the afternoon, guests were due to arrive at dinner to honor the visiting sister-in-law of one of Mrs. Nicholas's friends. John kept a close and eager eye on the dining room, his stomach rumbling in anticipation. The table had been set with a damask cloth and the family's best British china. At the left of each plate were a pair of silver forks, and at the right of each lay a knife, then a spoon turned upside down, its bowl rounded and shining.

Both Samson and Titus would be dressed in their best dark red livery and would remain in the room during the meal to serve from the sideboard.

First, there would be a soup course. John took a deep breath, enjoying the hint of fragrance slipping out from the covered tureen of beef broth that already wafted in from the butler's pantry. Five guests had been invited to the dinner, so with his family, there would be a total of twelve. One meat for every two people at the dinner party would be served, which meant six meats roasting on the spits: pork, beef, duck or goose, and venison. And perhaps there would be slices of baked chicken and ham. Since the next day April would turn into May, a month in which oysters would be at their best, it was likely oysters would also be served.

Titus had already placed a side dish to the left of each place in the dining room. Plates would be passed around the table until all had been served from every dish. John's mouth watered at the thought of the spiced peaches, stewed quinces, pickles, boiled carrots and beets, mincemeat pies, and custard. The meal would end with bowls of nuts and pieces of candied fruits.

John, standing between Wilson and Lewis, dutifully greeted his parents' guests as they arrived, then trailed behind them when they were invited to the dining room.

At the table, everyone enjoyed the food and spoke only of pleasant things.

Much later, his stomach tight as a drum, John rose with his brothers as his mother invited the women to join her in the parlor. Sighing, he wished he were old enough to remain with the men at the table, where they'd relax with glasses of wine and pipes.

Wilson, carrying a book, climbed the stairs. Lewis was right on Wilson's heels, but John hesitated. Even though he'd eaten his fill, there was still room for cake.

He sidled just inside the door to the parlor, where he was close to the coffee tray. Betsey, as the oldest unmarried daughter, took her place behind the table, where she prepared to pour coffee from a china pot. Betty stood nearby to serve queen's cake. John was certain he could count on Betty to see that he received a slice or two.

John had never paid much attention to what women spoke about at the parties his mother gave. He vaguely remembered snatches of conversations about gowns and hats and babies and ways to make lemon curd, so he was surprised to hear Mrs. Ashcroft say, "I hear John Randolph is considering taking his family back to England."

John Randolph—Edmund's father? John was surprised.

" 'Tis true," Mrs. Blair said. "John Randolph is seriously considering taking his family back to England."

John heard a gasp and turned to see the china pot waver in Betsey's hand. Drops of coffee spotted the linen cloth on the table. As she put the china pot down, her hands trembling, Betsey murmured tearfully, "I'm sorry, Mother. Pray excuse me."

" 'Tis but a drop. Betty will bring a clean cloth," Mrs. Nicholas answered.

"You are pale, child. Are you not well?" one of the guests asked Betsey.

"It is nothing. Pray excuse me," Betsey repeated. She rushed from the room without looking, and John had to jump back to keep from being run down.

Mrs. Roberts, the visiting guest, looked from Mrs. Blair to Mrs. Nicholas. "The news about John

Randolph seemed to upset Betsey. Is Edmund calling on her?"

Mrs. Nicholas moved to the empty chair behind the table and began to pour the coffee. "The day is warm. Betsey is merely feeling a touch of early summer's heat. A quiet rest will do her good."

Mrs. Blair smiled and said, "I've been wanting to ask about Sally. When is your daughter's baby expected?"

Mrs. Nicholas, sounding relieved that the subject had been changed, answered, "In July. It's hard to believe that little Courtenay is almost two."

As the women began to talk about babies, John left his post near the door and walked slowly up the stairs. He was no longer interested in cake. His mind was on what he had heard about John Randolph's taking his family back to England. Since Mr. Randolph was the head of the household, his minor children and unmarried daughters would have to follow his wishes, whether they were pleased with them or not.

John made a face. In the case of John Randolph, there would be orders, not wishes. But Edmund was twenty-two. He was no longer a child under his father's protection. Would Edmund go with his family? Or would he refuse?

John sat on the top step and rested his head in his hands. He thought about his own father, who had always been loyal to Great Britain. What if he, too, should decide to take his family back to England?

I'd have to leave my best friend and all the interesting, secret places around Williamsburg that Robert and I have discovered and made our own, he thought with dismay.

He'd be forced to leave his familiar home and live in a country he'd never seen. His sister Sally was married and would remain in Williamsburg with her husband if he chose to remain in Virginia. And, of course, George would never agree to go. George, at the age of twenty, was old enough to be independent.

John's eyes blurred, and a hot tear slid down the side of his nose. Fiercely, he rubbed it away with the back of one hand. *I'd never see George or Sally again,* he thought, and he shivered. This was *not* how he had imagined his life unfolding.

"I must talk to Father," John whispered into the shadows.

Later, after the guests had left, John found his father at his desk, reaching for a sheet of paper and a quill pen.

"Father," John began, "today I heard that Mr. John Randolph plans to take his family back to England."

Mr. Nicholas didn't look up from his paper. Dipping his quill into an ink pot, he began to write.

"Father," John tried again. "Mr. Randolph plans to—"

"Yes, John," Mr. Nicholas said as he continued to write. "I have no quarrel with Mr. Randolph's departure."

"His sympathies are with the Crown."

"That is his choice."

John waited a moment, then asked, "Will the army come here, sir?"

"Not if we can reach a reconciliation with our king and Parliament."

John took a sharp, deep breath and spilled out the question he'd been longing to ask: "You won't return to England, will you, Father?"

Mr. Nicholas kept writing, but he mumbled, "It is not a matter of my *returning* to England, since I have never resided in England. I was born here in Williamsburg."

"Does that mean we'll stay here in Williamsburg?"

Mr. Nicholas gave a long sigh, then raised his head and looked at John. "I have an important message to send, John. It is difficult for me to choose the correct words and answer your questions at the same time. May we discuss this later?"

"Yes, Father," John said. He turned and left the

room, discouraged that his father hadn't given him a definite answer. At least he hadn't said they *would* leave for England.

Through the side windows of the house, John could see George's company practicing maneuvers on the green near the Guardhouse and Magazine, practically across the street.

Pushing his worries aside, John ran to get Robert. If they stayed in Williamsburg and if an invasion was forthcoming, he and his best friend must prepare for it.

John and Robert found sturdy sticks about the size of muskets and rested them on their shoulders. They began to march in step behind the volunteers.

"Go home, lads," George called to them, but John shook his head.

"If we are to fight the British regulars, we must learn how," he answered.

"Let the lads be," someone shouted. "We may need all the help we can get."

Many of the young men laughed. George chuckled with them and gave no more orders to leave, so John and Robert stayed in place, copying the volunteers' every move.

When George finally called for a break, John flopped on the ground in relief. He stretched to take the ache from his left shoulder and elbow.

"Not so easy, is it, lad?" a man asked.

Robert, who had dropped down next to John, spoke up. "It's not easy at all. Why must we march until we're so tired?"

"An army spends many hours on its feet," the man answered. " 'Tis the way of it. If 'tis too much for you to manage, maybe you'd better wait a few years until you're old enough to keep up the pace."

A couple of young men who looked as if they still had a year or two to reach the age of twenty-one good-naturedly defended John and Robert. "I'm sure they will outmarch you, Silas, since you're an old man of thirty," one of them said.

"Ah, you're a fine one to talk, Beverley Dickson. You're not much older than they are," the man answered. "Are we to add babies' clouts to our company's supplies?"

Beverley and his friend Ben answered back good-naturedly. Everyone laughed, and the men were still joking when George called the company to order once more.

As dusk fell, the march ended. John stumbled home, thankful that he didn't have as far to go as Robert did. He sank into a chair, rubbing his aching shoulder, but soon Mary appeared, a smug smile on her face.

"We watched you and Robert playing soldier," she announced.

John looked up quickly. "Was Father angry?" he asked. "I must tell him that—"

"Father was not here. Mr. Pendleton came to talk to him about something. Then they both left to meet with Mr. Peyton Randolph. But before they left, I heard Mr. Pendleton say that those who fear an immediate invasion of Williamsburg are wrong."

John sighed with relief. But he soon remembered the conversation at dinner the day before. "*You* were one of the worriers," he accused his sister.

Mary sniffed. "I did not worry. I merely asked for information, which Father gave me."

"You asked George, not Father," John corrected.

Mary blushed, but she glared at John. "I don't remember *whom* I asked," she said. "In any case, Father was the one with the correct answer. As he told us, there is nothing to fear. It is over." She stalked off with a swish of petticoats.

John didn't try to answer his sister. He kept remembering George saying, "It's *not* over." If George was right, then there was good reason to be afraid of what might come.

"I need to talk to Father," John said to himself, but there was no way he could do so. His father was not at home.

Chapter Six

George had been right, John thought, when he'd said Williamsburg's troubles were not over. Two days later, on May 2, Patrick Henry, still angry about the theft of the gunpowder from the Williamsburg Magazine, organized his company of volunteers to march on Williamsburg.

That evening, he sent a small part of his company ahead to kidnap Richard Corbin, the receiver general, at his home in King and Queen County and force him to pay for the stolen powder from the king's revenues.

Mr. Nicholas was furious when a messenger arrived at his house early on the morning of Wednesday, May 3, with the news. "I cannot believe that Henry would be so bold as to attempt to kidnap one of the king's men!" he exclaimed to Mrs. Nicholas.

She pressed her fingertips to her cheeks and gasped, "Kidnapped?"

Mr. Nicholas went on to explain, "Thankfully, Corbin was not at home, so they were unable to capture him. Ironically enough, he is at the Governor's Palace attending a Council meeting called to deal with Mercer's threat, so he is out of harm's way."

John gave a jump of excitement. "Will Patrick Henry and his men march on the palace?"

"I pray they will not," Mr. Nicholas answered. He began to pace back and forth across the hall. "They are camped at Doncastle's Ordinary, which is only about fifteen miles from Williamsburg."

"That is not far, Father," John said, his heart beating faster. He was certain that George and James and their company would not be left out of any action taken in Williamsburg."

Mr. Nicholas smacked his right fist against his left palm. "Henry is a delegate to the Continental Congress, which is due to meet in just one week. Why can he not attend to the business before him, instead of meddling in action that could cause great harm?"

He groaned and added, "To make matters even worse, I was told that when the governor heard of Henry's attempt at kidnapping, he flew into a rage. He ordered forty marines and sailors from the *Fowey* to fortify the palace. And he repeated his threat to arm the slaves and spread devastation wherever he can reach."

So there will be fighting! John thought. *And George will be in it! And perhaps Samson and Titus will fight against him!* For a moment he found it hard to breathe.

John wondered if his mother had had the same thought, because she grew pale. "Husband, you *must* stop Patrick Henry," she demanded. "I fear that Governor Dunmore will do exactly as he threatens, and our son George . . ." She backed up and sat in one of the side chairs in the hall, apparently unable to continue.

Mr. Nicholas put an arm around his wife's shoulders. "Do not worry," he said. "I will ride to Doncastle's Ordinary and do what I can to stop Henry from actions that could endanger us all."

As he turned toward his bedchamber, he called out, "Samson! I will need my carriage!"

Mrs. Nicholas slowly pulled herself to her feet and followed her husband.

With neither of his parents paying attention to what he was doing, John dashed out the front door and across to the volunteers' encampment, where George and James had their heads bent together, deep in conversation.

By the time he had finished telling them what Mr. Nicholas had said, others had gathered.

"I say let Henry march on the palace," Beverley said. "With our company and others to join him, we'll show the governor we mean what we say!"

" 'Tis the best way to say it!" Ben said with a grin.

George nodded impatiently to John. "We know that Father will try to turn Patrick Henry away from Williamsburg," he said. "And you can be certain there are others who will ride with him to speak with Henry."

"Will they succeed in stopping him?" John asked.

"We can only wait and see," George answered. "But if Henry calls for reinforcements, our company is ready."

Benjamin, Ben, and the other men who had gathered around threw their hats in the air and shouted. "That we are!" Ben yelled. "We're ready for whatever may come!"

During the next two days, both confirmed news and rumor flew through Williamsburg. As talk grew of keeping the marines and sailors from entering Williamsburg, Captain George Montagu of the H.M.S. *Fowey* threatened to bombard Yorktown, where his ship was anchored.

"Does this not strain credulity?" Betsey asked at the dinner table that afternoon. "We are being treated like a foreign enemy, not like British citizens! Edmund says . . ."

As she broke off, glancing at her father's empty chair, Mrs. Nicholas frowned and said, "I fear that Edmund is very much like George in his desire for immediate action."

"George has told everyone that his volunteers will join Patrick Henry if he marches on Williamsburg," Mary said. She glanced at John. "At least we can be glad that Lewis, John, and Wilson are too young to fight."

Wilson looked up from his book and turned a page. "Fight? No. My brothers and I do not fight with each other," he said. "Fighting and squabbles are pointless." He went back to reading.

Betsey spoke softly. "Mother, Sally sent a note to me this morning. Her husband, John, hopes to be elected captain of the Williamsburg militia."

"John has a very young daughter and will soon be father to a second child," Mary said, a woeful expression on her face. "He should continue serving as justice of the peace and not be leading a militia company. It is bad enough that George might be involved in fighting."

Mrs. Nicholas gave each of her children a stern look. "We cannot tell John Norton what to do. And let us not indulge in any further talk of George's volunteer company's becoming involved in fighting," she said. "Your father is now doing his best to convince Mr. Henry to disband *his* company and travel to Philadelphia to the Congress, where he belongs."

The moment the meal was over and they were all excused from the table, John left the house. No one had forbidden him to practice marching with George's company, so he intended to continue.

John and Robert worked twice as long and hard as they had before, and John sometimes imagined he was marching as a real soldier toward a real battle.

He enjoyed sitting with Beverley and Ben and some of the younger men in the company. They had many good stories to tell. Some, like the tale of the man who tried to ride a pig home from market, caused John and everyone around him to roar with laughter. Some stories, such as one about the ghost who haunted a patch of woods near Yorktown, were so scary they made John hunch forward, curling his toes. But he especially liked hearing Ben and Beverley tell stories about their boyhoods and their families. Even though both young men were in their twenties, John felt that age didn't matter. They were still his—and Robert's—good friends.

On the evening of May 5, Mr. Nicholas returned home, dusty and weary, with news about Richard Corbin's son-in-law, Carter Braxton. Braxton had convinced Henry to call a truce while he arranged to pay for the powder. Henry had refused his offer, but instead accepted payment of the same amount from a merchant-planter in Yorktown.

"Henry promised to buy more powder for the Magazine with the money," Mr. Nicholas said with a scowl. "Then, the man boldly offered to continue into Williamsburg with his troops to guard the public treasury. Of course, as treasurer, I refused him."

John knew he shouldn't interrupt, but he couldn't wait to find out. "Will Patrick Henry and his volunteers come to Williamsburg, Father?"

Mr. Nicholas looked at John as though for a moment he'd forgotten he was there. "No, Son. He listened to reason and dismissed his troops, sending them home. He then headed his horse toward Philadelphia, which is what he should have done in the first place."

"I pray he will arrive safely," Mrs. Nicholas murmured.

The corners of Mr. Nicholas's mouth turned down in a wry smile. "Have no fear on that account," he said. "Three companies in full dress volunteered to escort Henry to the Maryland border, where he'd then be safe." He dropped his chin and grumbled, "I'm afraid that many of the people of Virginia mistakenly think of Henry as a hero."

Mrs. Nicholas placed a hand on his arm. "*You* are the hero, Husband. You helped avert what could have been a great tragedy."

Mr. Nicholas stood a little straighter as he said, "I have been talking to Carter Braxton. We are both in agreement that at the next convention Henry should be censured."

Mrs. Nicholas nodded, but John wasn't sure he agreed with his father. It was true that Patrick Henry was outspoken. Perhaps his actions had disturbed those who still believed disagreements with the Crown could be solved peacefully, but he had succeeded in obtaining payment for the stolen powder, hadn't he? Others had felt it was useless to try or had been afraid to anger Lord Dunmore, but Mr. Henry had acted on what he believed.

I think Patrick Henry is a hero, too, John thought, and hoped that he would not be censured at convention.

Patrick Henry, Mr. Nicholas, Peyton Randolph, George, Hugh Mercer, and others who were trying to maintain Virginia's rights under the British government were taking many different paths to reach that goal. But couldn't they see, John wondered, that even though they had chosen different directions, they were all working to win the same results?

On May 12, Governor Dunmore brought his family back to the palace and sent the guard from the *Fowey* to their ship. Then he issued a proclamation that the General Assembly meet on June 1.

During a break in the volunteer company's training, John heard George tell Captain Innes, "Dunmore expects the burgesses to agree to Prime Minister Lord North's proposal concerning taxation in the colonies. He calls it a means to a peaceful reconciliation."

John was surprised. Had their father been right about peaceful means being the best way after all? John realized that he wasn't the only one in Williamsburg who had been greatly relieved when Lady Dunmore and her children returned to the palace. Everyone was certain it meant there was no threat of invasion. And perhaps the British government and the colonies were moving closer to a reconciliation. Wasn't that the reason for a discussion of Lord North's peaceful proposal?

Even though he wasn't part of the conversation, John stepped up to George, with Robert right behind him. "Does that mean that the king and Parliament will guarantee the colonists their rights as British citizens?" John asked.

George shook his head. "We have seen North's proposal. It promises not to tax the colonists if they will agree to tax themselves, but—"

"That is what we have asked for!" John interrupted.

"Hear me out," George told him. "The taxes must be in line with quotas sent to us by Parliament."

"Quotas?" Robert looked puzzled. "Does that mean we still will be told what the taxes should be?"

John thought a moment. "Yes. It means the taxes will be just as heavy."

George agreed. "If the proposal is approved, we will still have the high taxes, but we will not be able to blame Parliament for them."

"Surely the burgesses won't agree to the proposal, will they?" John asked.

George shrugged. "I hope they will have the good sense not to," he answered.

Beverley Dickson joined the group. His face had reddened, and he spoke quietly. "I couldn't help hearing what you were saying, and I'd like to add my piece."

George smiled. "Far be it from us to deny a man his say."

Beverley took a long breath, and his words tumbled out. "Well then," he said, "in the opinion of some of us, the governor is trying to trick the burgesses into coming into Williamsburg, where he can seize them. Then it's off to one of the British ships they'll go, where they'll be carried across the sea to London courts and prison."

John gasped aloud. He could see that Robert's face

was drawn with fear. They moved so close together, John could feel Robert tremble. Or was it he himself who was shaking so fearfully?

"Father is a burgess," John whispered. "Could that happen to him?"

George slapped a hand on his shoulder. "Don't worry about Father," he reassured him. "Don't worry about the burgesses. We will not let any of them be captured or imprisoned."

Captain James Innes said, "There are many in Williamsburg who mistrust our governor."

"With good reason," Beverley added.

Captain Innes put an arm around Beverley's shoulders. "I have made up my mind. It is time for us to issue a statement that we are ready to resist the landing of British troops in Virginia or anywhere else on the continent."

George nodded firmly. "Provided we do not leave our own colony defenseless."

James said, "It's important that the governor and others know that we will consider the landing of foreign troops in Virginia a dangerous attack on liberty." He paused, then added, "We will resist such measures at the expense of life and fortune."

"Of life and fortune," Beverley echoed.

"So be it," George said.

Captain Innes's statement circulated around the town in early June. John heard from a number of sources that the governor was highly irritated at this "act of defiance," as he called it, but he did not take action against Captain Innes.

Robert Carter Nicholas, however, was open in his criticism of Captain Innes's statement. "Does that young man have any idea of what is meant by 'at the expense of life and fortune'?" he asked.

"I'm afraid not," Mrs. Nicholas murmured.

"I do not know," Mary said.

Wilson raised his head from his book. "Life and fortune are separate concepts and should have no relationship to each other," he said. He returned to his book.

John looked questioningly at Mr. Nicholas. "I think it means we will fight even if we die and spend all our money," he answered. "Pray explain it, Father, so that we may understand."

Mr. Nicholas scowled. "Why should these young men like Captain James Innes and George so willingly take action that might cost us dearly?" he asked. "There are better ways to win the concessions we seek." He walked off, still angrily mumbling to himself.

"I still don't understand all that it means," John complained, but his father had left the room and no one else answered him.

Chapter Seven

During the last week of May, John awoke early each morning, concerned about what the day would bring. Might Captain Innes and his volunteers engage the sailors and marines from the *Fowey* in battle? Would drumbeats again sound a sudden alarm?

To John's surprise, the last week of May passed quietly and without incident. On May 24, Peyton Randolph turned his post as president of the Continental Congress over to John Hancock. It took almost a week for Mr. Randolph to travel to Williamsburg, where he was needed as Speaker of the House of Burgesses.

He was escorted with great ceremony into Williamsburg by volunteers from Captain Innes's company. Although George forbade John and Robert to march with the volunteers, they proudly ran alongside the detachment, weaving through the crowd that had turned out to cheer them.

The next morning, John and Robert were again on hand when some of the company marched to Mr. Randolph's front door and posted a protective guard.

John rejoiced at seeing his friends Beverley and Ben in the guard. He nudged Robert and grinned as he said, "We aren't going to let even one of Captain Montagu's marines set foot near Mr. Randolph!"

"You don't mean *marines*. You mean *boiled crabs*!" Robert yelled, and bent over laughing. "Mr. Purdie's *Virginia Gazette* called the marines 'boiled crabs'!"

On the morning of June 1, John and Robert joined a large group of people who eagerly flocked to the Capitol to hear and see what would take place at this opening session of the General Assembly.

Robert plucked at John's sleeve as they squeezed through the crowd for a better view. "Do you see Thomas Jefferson?" he asked. "My father said he had come to make sure Lord North's proposal would be voted down."

"I don't see him," John said. "Maybe he has already entered the Capitol."

Robert shouted, "Look! Two of the burgesses are wearing hunting shirts like the ones the volunteer soldiers wear! And there's another one . . . and another. And each carries a tomahawk at his belt!"

John jumped with excitement. Perhaps his father would wear a hunting shirt, too!

But Robert Carter Nicholas soon appeared, head held high as he strode into the Capitol at the side of James Mercer. Both men were dressed in their usual dark wool frock coats and breeches, white ruffled shirts, and cocked hats. John saw his father cast a sharp, disapproving look at the hunting shirt of one of his fellow burgesses.

John fought down a surge of disappointment. *I should have known that Father could only be . . . well . . . Father,* he thought.

"What do you think the burgesses will do?" Robert asked.

"Some of them want to dismiss Lord North's proposal the very first thing," John answered, "but Father insists that the burgesses must at least discuss the proposal."

"What is there to discuss, if the proposal is wrong?"

Embarrassed because he didn't understand the reason himself, John said, "Father says you have to discuss a matter if you want to be fair."

"Even if you know you'll vote against it?"

Grumpily, John exclaimed, "Stop asking questions, Robert! I don't know."

Robert didn't give up. "How will your father vote on the proposal?" he asked.

"I don't know that, either!" John shouted. He slunk back as a few people turned to stare at him. He wished he hadn't shouted. He wished he knew what his father intended to do. He wished he understood who was right—his father or his brother George.

"I hope they will vote on Lord North's proposal soon," Robert said. "I don't want to stand out here all day."

A man turned to Robert with a chuckle. "Lad, 'tis not likely the burgesses will get to voting on *anything* till next week. For one thing, there's roll call. Then there are speeches to be made and points of order to discuss. No government body ever gets right to the business of things."

There was loud laughter around them, and voices raised in agreement.

John, his disappointment growing, whispered to Robert, "If nothing exciting is going to happen, let's go back to the Magazine and march with the volunteers. We can ask Beverley what it was like guarding the Speaker of the House."

The volunteers were at rest when John and Robert

arrived. John looked for Beverley and didn't see him, so he asked someone nearby, "Do you know where we can find Beverley or Ben?"

The man jerked a thumb toward the nearby Guardhouse. "Not long ago I seen Ben walkin' around the other side."

"Thank you," John said. He and Robert followed Ben's route.

But as John reached the porch of the Guardhouse, he could hear Beverley's voice coming from just around the corner.

"My sister got a letter from a friend in Georgia. She said patriots there broke into the public magazine and seized the powder."

"Patriots? Not British soldiers?" John recognized Ben's voice.

"Patriots, as I said," Beverley went on. "I've been thinking about what they did, and it seems a right good idea. Here in Williamsburg, I expect that the royal marines will come back for the rest of the guns and powder just as soon as the burgesses vote down Lord North's proposal."

John stopped, startled by Beverley's statement.

"Are you certain they'll vote it down?" Ben asked.

"I'm certain, as is everyone else in Virginia. They'll have to discuss the proposal, because that's what burgesses think they must do, but their vote will mostly be against it. Then Governor Dunmore will have a fit of anger and threaten everyone again."

"And that's when you think the royal marines will be ordered to steal what's left in the Magazine?"

"Unless we break in and take it first." There was a pause. Then Beverley said, "I know how to open the lock without a key."

John tried to smother the gasp that rose in his throat. He flattened himself against the wall and saw that Robert had done the same. This was a conversation they should not be overhearing, but John couldn't leave. Not yet.

John's first thought was that Beverley and Ben were fools to try to save the guns and powder from the British marines. They could be arrested and thrown into the gaol. But he soon began to think that perhaps they were not so foolish. Instead, they seemed brave enough to do what needed to be done to protect the people of Williamsburg. What they planned to do had been done before. In Georgia. Beverley had said so.

"Rafe will be with us," he heard Beverley say.

"Then it will be the three of us," Ben answered. "When will we do it?"

"I heard that the burgesses will discuss the proposal this week, so nothing will be done until Monday. We must do what we can before then."

"Do you mean tonight?"

"No. Saturday night will be best. Half after midnight, when most people are in their beds."

"What about the night watch? When does he make his rounds?"

"He comes past the Magazine the same time each night—between eleven-fifty and midnight. He'll present no difficulty."

A whistle sounded, signaling the end of the rest period, and Beverley's voice grew suddenly louder, as if he was turning toward them.

"We'll meet at the Magazine at twelve-thirty," he said.

John grabbed Robert's arm and raced around the opposite corner of the Guardhouse. He didn't stop until he and Robert were well out of sight. Thankful they hadn't been seen, he dropped to the ground, panting.

Robert plopped down beside him. "Can you believe it? Ben and Beverley and Rafe are going to steal the supplies that are left in the Magazine!" he said, his voice shaking.

"Not *steal*," John insisted. "They're going to keep the marines from taking the armaments. They're going to save the people of Williamsburg."

Robert cocked his head, studying John. "Will you tell George?" he asked.

"No," John said. " 'Tis Beverley's secret—his and Ben's and Rafe's." He thought a moment and added with growing excitement, "And ours. Robert, we can be there, too."

Robert stiffened. "At half past midnight? I'm always asleep at half past midnight."

John sighed and said, "Then I'll go alone."

"In the dark? In the middle of the night?"

Shaking his head, John said, "Robert, we're too old for goblins and being scared of the dark. We're old enough to be soldiers, and we can prove it to George when we tell him we helped take the powder and guns and hide them from the governor and the royal ma—" He smiled and said, "from the boiled crabs."

"Count me in," Robert said. He held out a hand and John solemnly shook it. "You and I will help defend Virginia, too."

In the overnight hours between Saturday, June 3, and Sunday, June 4, John crept from his bed, down the stairs, and out the front door. A smattering of clouds drifted over the thin moon, shifting the night sky in and out of total darkness. Guided only by these brief glimpses of light, John cautiously made his way across Francis Street. Within minutes, the Guardhouse loomed up before him, and just beyond rose the high brick wall that surrounded the octagonal Magazine.

As John waited, straining to see, the shadows at the base of the Magazine seemed to stretch and move. Ice slid down his backbone, and he shivered, suddenly remembering all the scary tales of headless creatures and avenging ghosts George had told him on cold, dark nights.

He sagged against one of the posts that supported the roof of the Guardhouse and tried to breathe slowly and steadily. The shadows became clearer, and he realized that they were shadows of men who were moving along the wall toward the north entrance of the Magazine.

A hand clutched John's arm, and his mouth flew open. He tried to cry out, but he was too frightened to make more than a low gurgling sound.

"*Hsst!* John, it's only me," Robert whispered.

John gripped the post, resting his head against it for a moment until his heartbeat slowed to near normal. "They're here," he managed to say. "They've already moved to the other side of the Magazine. Hurry! We'll be late!"

He ran across the grass, occasionally stumbling in his eagerness to be with Beverley, Ben, and Rafe as they entered the Magazine. John knew there were rows of rifles stored around the walls, and he planned to fill his arms with them, carrying them to wherever Beverley intended to hide them.

The boys had entered the door in the wall. There were sounds of metal scraping against metal at the lock in the Magazine. *With the light in their lantern covered so they won't be seen, they must be having trouble opening the lock,* John thought. "We're in time!" he said aloud, and dashed forward.

Without warning, he stumbled over uneven ground and landed facedown, smacking his chin hard. As he tried to rise, rubbing his aching chin, Robert, who was close behind him, tripped and fell on top of him.

"Climb off! Move! Hurry!" John grunted. He tried to push Robert out of the way, which caused an even greater tangle of arms and legs.

"Let go!" Robert said through his teeth. "I can stand up, if you give me half a chance!"

John groaned in frustration as he heard the heavy wooden door of the Magazine begin to creak open. He managed to scramble to his feet, but he stopped, frozen in surprise at the sound of a shot that came from inside the Magazine.

As fast as he could, John ran through the open door, stopping short. In the flickering light of the lantern, which lay exposed on its side, he saw Beverley, Ben, and Rafe on the ground.

Ben held his arm, rocking back and forth, groaning in pain.

Rafe whimpered, "I'm shot. I'm bleeding." He stared with amazement at his bloody right hand, from which two fingers were missing.

Beverley lay on his back, as still as if he were sleeping, his arms outspread.

There was no sign of whoever had shot them. He must have fled, John decided. Or could he be hiding in the Magazine? No! John didn't want to think about that, and he had no time to waste searching. He gripped Robert's shoulders. "Run for help!" he shouted. "Run to my house! It's close by! Tell Samson to fetch a doctor and raise an alarm!"

As Robert turned, disappearing in a flash, John dropped to his knees beside Beverley. Blood from a wound on the side of his head oozed down his neck, soaking into the ground.

Even though Beverley didn't open his eyes, he let out a low groan. John, who felt as frozen as pond ice in January, responded to the groan with relief. Beverley *wasn't* dead. But he needed help.

As John desperately tried to think of what he could do, he remembered his mother applying pressure to a bleeding cut on his knee when he was younger and had fallen out of a tree. Apply pressure.

He could do that. But he would need a clean cloth. He couldn't wait for a cloth to be brought. There wasn't time. Where could he find a clean cloth?

John pulled off his shirt and tore it, folding the strips into thick pads. He pressed the pads against the wound, hoping and praying the bleeding would stop.

This is war, he thought with a shudder, *and war means death.* Beverley could die. George could die. Maybe he and Robert could die. Bile rose in John's throat and he forced it back, choking and gagging. Suddenly, the words of Patrick Henry's speech became all too clear to John: "Give me liberty or give me death." *This* was the death Patrick Henry spoke of, the death John feared—and yet, it was the price Beverley, George, and the rest of the militia were willing to pay. Was liberty really worth giving one's life for? John hoped none of them would have to pay such a price.

A man knelt beside John, the light from his lantern casting wavering shadows across the enclosure. When John saw that it was Dr. James Carter, he breathed a long sigh of relief.

"Good work, lad," the doctor said. "Move aside now, so I can see what this young man needs."

"His name is Beverley Dickson," John said. He was surprised to discover that he was crying.

As he moved out of the doctor's way, he was jostled by the night watch, who rushed in, his lantern held high.

"A spring gun! A loaded shotgun with a spring to trip it!" the man shouted. "See! It was set to fire upon anyone opening the door to the Magazine."

Now there were many voices, most of them raised in anger. "Assassins!" "Murderers!" "Dunmore's to blame!" "Who would believe he'd set a trap to kill our youth!"

John put his hands to his head, wishing he were in his bed and all this were nothing more than a very bad dream.

Chapter Eight

Strong hands gripped John's shoulders and pulled him to his feet. "Come with me, Son," Mr. Nicholas said.

John leaned against his father as they made their way back across Francis Street to their home. "Robert?" he asked. "Where is Robert?"

"With his parents, where he should have been all along," Mr. Nicholas answered.

"Robert and I only wished to help save the armaments," John tried to explain. " 'Twas what patriots in Georgia did to save their arms. They broke into their magazine and hid the guns and powder from the British militia. Beverley said so."

He broke off, stumbling over the doorstep as they entered their house. "Father, will Beverley die?"

"I heard Dr. Carter say that two of the young men have minor wounds. He hoped that the third would recover quickly."

"John! Oh, John!" Mrs. Nicholas cried. As John dropped into the nearest chair, Diana appeared with a basin of water and a cloth. Mrs. Nicholas knelt beside John and began to wipe the blood from his hands.

John was aware that Betsey, Mary, Wilson, and Lewis were in the hall, their faces pale and shadowy in the candlelight. But he spoke only to his father, telling him all that had happened.

When he had finished, Mr. Nicholas said, "A gun loaded with shot was rigged to discharge when the Magazine door was opened."

"Why?" Wilson asked in amazement. "Who would do such a thing?"

"Governor Dunmore! That's who would order such a devilish plot!" Mrs. Nicholas snapped. She softly stroked John's forehead, but her voice was firm. "Do you realize that you and Robert could have been killed?"

"No one was killed, Mother," John tried to explain.

The door burst open, and George entered, his clothes mussed and his hair uncombed. "I heard what happened," he said. "Is John—"

"I am not hurt," John said. "Neither is Robert."

"They should not have been at the Magazine!"

Mrs. Nicholas's voice was still filled with worry and anger.

"Perhaps not," George said, "but it was well they were on hand. I was told that John saved young Beverley Dickson's life."

John sat upright, his heart giving an extra thump. "I did? Beverley will not die?"

George stepped forward and gripped John's shoulder. "You stopped the bleeding. If not attended to, Beverley could have bled to death. If infection does not develop, Dr. Carter thinks he will recover completely." He tried to look stern. "However, I am not saying you *should* have joined those lads. 'Twas a foolhardy risk."

"But in Georgia—"

"I know about Georgia." George smiled as he added, "And I can't help thinking 'twould have really tweaked Dunwoody's nose if the boiled crabs had gone to get the rest of the armaments and found them missing!"

Mr. Nicholas cleared his throat loudly, then said, "George, surely you can now see the wrong example you have set for your brothers."

George looked surprised. "I had nothing to do with the break-in at the Magazine," he said.

"Tonight's tragedy is but one example," Mr. Nicholas told him. "Hotheaded words and actions—"

George interrupted, anger edging his words.

"Leading and training volunteer soldiers is hardly a hotheaded action. We may represent your only safety during the coming months. We are even now mobilizing to protect the Magazine. We have more than two hundred volunteers arriving, and we'll keep them here until the threat of imminent danger is over."

The argument grew louder. John saw his sisters and brothers disappear like wisps of smoke up the darkened stairway. He stopped listening to what his father and brother were shouting at each other. He wrapped his arms around his shoulders, ducking his head. He didn't like to hear George and his father so angry. He agreed with some of the things his father said, and he agreed with most of the things George said. But his thoughts were in a muddle. The British had almost killed Beverley! Would they attack more volunteers and finally start a war? What might happen to his family? What might happen to the people who lived in Williamsburg? In Virginia? In the colonies? He couldn't begin to guess.

Over the next few days, everywhere John went, he heard angry accusations about the spring gun set at the Magazine. Mr. Alexander Purdie, editor of one of the three *Virginia Gazette* newspapers, angrily wrote that if any of the wounded should die, whoever was responsible for setting the gun would deserve to be called a murderer. And Mr. Nicholas's friend, Edmund Pendleton, who was attending the Continental Congress in Philadelphia, angrily proclaimed that the assassination of Governor Dunmore might be in order.

On Monday morning, a mob stormed the Magazine but was unable to enter. On Monday afternoon, a committee of burgesses visited Governor Dunmore, asking for the keys to the Magazine so that they might investigate the shooting.

Mr. Robert Carter Nicholas was a member of that group, and he later reported the meeting to his family. Governor Dunmore had become so furious that the veins in his neck bulged and his face turned purple.

"Did he give you the keys, Father?" John asked. He remembered that Beverley, not having the authority or dignity of a burgess, hadn't needed a key to break into the Magazine.

Mr. Nicholas scowled. "Dunmore did not. He demanded we give him a request in writing. So we left one with him. We hope we will receive an answer from him tomorrow."

Mrs. Nicholas gasped. "You have a right to conduct an investigation. How could he possibly have given that response?"

"He is a vengeful, spiteful man," Mr. Nicholas said.

"If it were not for Dunmore and others like him, I am certain we could reach the king with our appeals and he would listen to reason."

It was hard for John to believe what he was hearing. George was mobilizing volunteers and the people of Williamsburg were showing their anger at what Governor Dunmore had done, but his father still hoped that peaceful discussions could solve the colonies' many problems.

"Father," John said, "there is much I don't understand. Will you—"

Mr. Nicholas interrupted. "John, at your age all you need to understand is that you must study your lessons well, keep a good heart by being kind and charitable to all, and obey God and your parents."

"But I wish to ask—"

Mr. Nicholas reached for his cloak and called out, "Samson!"

"Father, if you could but listen to my questions," John began.

Mr. Nicholas sighed. He rested his hands on John's shoulders and bent to look into his eyes. "Son," he said, "these are difficult times, and I must go where I am needed. We will soon vote on Lord North's proposal, and 'tis up to me and those of like mind to calm the burgesses, whose approach to the discussion is likely to be rash and imprudent. Do you understand?"

"Yes, Father," John answered. He tried his best to understand, but he couldn't help wishing that his father wasn't too busy to have time for his own son.

On Tuesday, Captain George Montagu of the *Fowey* offered to send one hundred marines to aid Governor Dunmore. On hearing this, Captain James Innes called his company to prepare for action. The House of Burgesses, still angered by Governor Dunmore's rude treatment of their committee, officially requested that Captain Innes and his volunteers guard the Magazine.

It surprised John—and the people of Williamsburg—when Governor Dunmore apologized to the burgesses for what he called "a misunderstanding" about the keys. It was even more surprising when he offered to return the powder taken from the Magazine.

He made an appointment to meet the assembly of burgesses on Thursday, June 8, and led them to believe that he would at that time formally apologize for the incident with the spring gun.

Mr. Nicholas remarked to his family, "At last it seems that the governor and the House of Burgesses may conduct a truly peaceful discussion. I hope it will bring an end to the conflicts that have arisen in Williamsburg."

But instead of meeting with the burgesses, at two in the morning on June 8, Governor Dunmore, his aides, and his family slipped quietly out of the palace and escaped to the H.M.S. *Magdalen,* which had been anchored for a few days in Queen's Creek.

Rumor had it that the governor had complained that his house was threatened every night with assault, and he feared for his life.

But once John saw that day's publication of John Pinkney's *Virginia Gazette,* he guessed the true reason Governor Dunmore had left. The newspaper printed a shocking letter the governor had sent to Lord Dartmouth, the British secretary of state for the colonies, the past December, in which he had requested a "blockading squadron."

"A blockading squadron? Why would Dunmore want to blockade us?" Mrs. Nicholas looked shocked upon hearing the news. She seated herself at the table, which had been set for the midday meal.

The blessing was short, and Betsey was quick to answer. "The sloop H.M.S. *Otter* and the schooner *Arundel* appeared recently in the York River," she said. "Edmund suspects they are to take part in an invasion!"

She leaned forward in her chair, eager to impart the latest news. "Edmund pointed out that Governor Josiah Martin of North Carolina fled the colonies less than two weeks ago. He heard this from Mr. Purdie, who intends to write about it in his next *Virginia Gazette*."

John looked from Betsey to his father, whose drawn face showed his deep concern about what was taking place. Mr. Nicholas looked up at Betsey's use of Edmund's name, and Betsey blushed.

"Father," she said, "you and Edmund have the same love of Virginia and the same desire to be guaranteed full British liberties. Edmund has told me that his father may leave Virginia for England, but he will stay. His fear is that his father's conduct may damage people's opinion of him."

"Edmund is a fine young man," Mrs. Nicholas said softly. "It would be wrong for anyone to judge Edmund and his father together."

Mr. Nicholas nodded, his eyes sad as he looked at Betsey. "Your mother is correct. I have given Edmund permission to call on you, Daughter," he said.

Betsey's face shone. She giggled and murmured, "I thank you, Father!"

She looked as if she had much more to say, but John had more important things on his mind than giggling sisters. "Father, how goes it with

Governor Dunmore? Will he soon return to Williamsburg?"

Mr. Nicholas served the last plate. His voice was touched with bitterness as he said, "Governor Dunmore, in his complaints to London, has lumped us all together—those of us who are trying to negotiate with peaceful means and those who are known firebrands, like Patrick Henry. How can anyone deal with a man who thinks like that?"

Mrs. Nicholas sighed. "Is there nothing you can do, Husband?"

In a weary voice, Mr. Nicholas answered, "Do not sound so hopeless, madam. Things *can* be done. For one, I am chairing a committee of burgesses to investigate the reasons for the governor's flight. I'm certain if we question every witness we can find, we will prove that Virginians on the whole have tried their best to keep the peace."

John wondered if his father was going to ignore people like Richard Bland, who had returned from Congress urging that Governor Dunmore be hanged, or Edmund Pendleton, who had suggested that Dunmore be assassinated. Or would his committee interview only witnesses who shared the viewpoint that all Virginians were reasonable and calm?

Mr. Nicholas paused only a moment, lowering his voice, before he added, "As treasurer, I have purchased for our Virginia colony five thousand pounds' worth of gunpowder. I have arranged with John Goodrich, a sea captain from Portsmouth, to bring it to Williamsburg."

"Father!" John exclaimed, dropping both his fork and napkin in his excitement. "You have joined the fight!"

"I have done no such thing," Mr. Nicholas answered. "I have merely made it possible for the colony of Virginia to protect itself." He cleared his throat and added, "The House of Burgesses is carrying on its usual routine, behaving as if the governor is fulfilling his royal duties. We have requested standard supplies for two thousand stands of arms, five tons of powder, and twenty tons of lead to restock the Magazine. We have also asked if we might distribute to the volunteer companies the arms mounted in the hallway of the palace."

John tried to keep his mouth from falling open in amazement. Finally, he was able to ask, "How did the governor answer, Father?"

"We do not expect him to answer immediately," Mr. Nicholas said. He turned to Mrs. Nicholas. "Pray excuse me, madam. I must meet with my committee before the afternoon session of the assembly convenes."

"Can you not stay a little longer, Husband?" she coaxed. "You have barely touched your meal, and we have boiled custard for dessert. 'Tis a favorite of yours."

"Jefferson is eager to get back to the Congress in Philadelphia," he said. We have much work to finish so that a vote on Lord North's proposal can be taken soon. We hope this can be accomplished within a day or two."

John ate quickly. He planned to meet Robert at the Magazine and continue to train with the volunteers. No one had yet told them they couldn't.

As he arrived at the Magazine, he saw that Ben and Rafe had returned, bandaged but up on their feet. And when the volunteers were at rest, both Yorktown men carried the message to John that Beverley was healing fast and would soon return to duty.

But something puzzled John. George had not objected when John and Robert took their places in the last ranks of the marchers. John had expected his brother to order him home, but he didn't. He seemed distracted, as if something far more important than a younger brother was on his mind.

"George gets like this when he is planning something," John confided to Robert. "I have seen him behave like this many times, so I am certain."

"What is he planning?" Robert asked.

"That I do not know," John answered. He glanced over at George. "But I intend to keep an eye on him. Somehow, I'm going to find out what he has in mind."

Chapter Nine

George was not often home during the next few days, so it was hard for John to learn what was occupying his brother's thoughts. Yet each time John saw George with his volunteer company, he became more and more certain that something was being planned. What it could be was a complete mystery to John.

"Dunmore has yet to reply," John heard George say to Captain Innes.

Reply about what? John wondered. Did this have anything to do with what George was planning? But George said nothing else that could give John a clue.

Word was sent to Williamsburg that the Continental Congress, meeting in Philadelphia, had established the Continental Army on June 14, and the next day had unanimously chosen George Washington to be the army's commander in chief.

"Edmond said we are moving closer to revolution," Betsey informed the Nicholas family at supper that evening.

Mr. Nicholas looked weary as he answered, "There is no need for a revolution. I insist that a satisfactory compromise can be reached between the colonies and Great Britain if we but continue to try."

"How long should we try, Father?" Mary asked.

Mr. Nicholas slowly shook his head. "As long as necessary," he answered.

"Governor Dunmore is both angry and afraid," Mary persisted. "He has repeated his threats. What if he should make them good?"

Betsey sat up straighter. "Edmund said he will," she said, and proudly began to repeat Edmund Randolph's latest opinion.

But John happened to look up in time to catch the strange look Titus gave Mr. Nicholas. It lasted not more than two seconds before Titus lowered his gaze and stood obediently next to the sideboard, waiting to perform any work asked of him.

The look frightened John. It seemed to be a flash of defiance mixed with excitement. *Titus will leave to fight with the British, as will Samson,* John thought. *There is no doubt about it.* For an instant, he felt weak with fear as he wondered how they would go. Would it be a quiet disappearance in the dark of night? Or would they cause destruction in the Nicholas household before they left?

"Father," John suddenly said aloud, "I am afraid."

Everyone in his family turned to look at him.

"Dear child, your father will take care of us. There is nothing to be afraid of," Mrs. Nicholas soothed.

But Mr. Nicholas looked at John with eyes full of sorrow. "Unfortunately, John, we must all be afraid of what is to come," he said.

Betsey glanced at John with sympathy. "Just remember that Edmund said . . ."

John didn't listen. At the moment he didn't care what Edmund or anyone else had to say. Everything he had ever known was changing, and he had no idea what would happen next.

On June 22, the members of the House received word from Governor Dunmore that on no condition would he give permission to the burgesses to take possession of the arms stored in the entrance hall of the Governor's Palace.

At supper that night, George joined the family, and he complained to his father, "How could the burgesses not vote to seize the arms after Dunmore refused to turn them over?"

"A rash action does not solve difficulties," Mr. Nicholas said. " 'Tis true, however, that the vote unfortunately carried by only a slim majority."

George's eyes sparkled. "Of which you were one, no doubt, Father."

"There is no need to discuss my position, George."

"Nor mine, Father. Not taking the arms did a great disservice to our Virginia colonists. We have not enough arms for our company, let alone for those who need protection." George leaned forward intently. "You have seen the vast store of arms in the Governor's Palace," he said.

"*I* haven't," John piped up. "Are they in stacks? In boxes?"

George smiled. "No, at present, muskets and pistols are arranged in patterns around the wood-paneled walls and in a great circle on the ceiling, bayonets at the center. At the sides of each doorway, swords are hung in a crossed design, and there are rows of muskets pointing upward around the room. A great many weapons are also stored along the stairwell."

"Why?" John asked. It was hard for him to imagine why rooms and stairwells should be decorated with weapons.

"When Alexander Spotswood was governor of

Virginia, around fifty years ago, he thought a show of arms would impress visitors with his power as representative of the British Crown," George said. "Governors since Spotswood did not see fit to make a change in the decoration."

"Enough of that." Mr. Nicholas shifted impatiently. He began to explain to George the legal ownership of the arms, but John didn't pay attention. It was obvious to him that George was no longer lost in deep thought. George was as alert as a house cat ready to pounce on a mouse. And he had said "at present" when he spoke of the armaments.

John sucked in his breath, and his heart gave a thump of excitement. He knew what had been on George's mind. He knew what George was planning to do.

Mr. Nicholas finished his argument. "So you can see 'twas a wise move to vote against seizing the armaments in the palace."

The meal began, and George bent to his soup, not answering. But John knew that George's answer would not be talk. It would be action.

Was action the best course? It had only led to injury at the Magazine a few weeks earlier. Still, John knew he needed to do *something*. *When George and his men take the arms from the palace, I plan to be there,* John decided.

John was certain that the raid, when it happened, would take place during the dark of night, and he tried to work out a plan in which he would remain awake, sneaking to the area where George's volunteers were camped. There he could keep an eye on George's tent.

"When?" Robert asked as soon as John told him the plan.

"Tonight," John said.

"I can't go at night." Robert made a face of disgust. "My father was so angry that we had gone to the Magazine the night of the shooting, he ordered me not to leave the house after dark."

"For how long?"

"For the rest of my life."

"Then I'll keep watch myself," John insisted.

His younger brother Lewis was no help, either.

"I will not be scolded again for helping you," Lewis said. He made a face at John.

"Even if I let you keep my pocketknife again for a week . . . *two* weeks?"

Lewis faltered but finally shook his head, his voice firm as he answered, "No. Mama made me promise I would not help you deceive her again."

Indignantly, John said, "I am not deceiving or disobeying anyone. No one has told me I cannot keep a watch on George."

Lewis's lower lip curled out. "No," he said stubbornly. "I will not help you."

"Then I'll do it myself," John said. He climbed into bed, determined to leave as soon as his mother had come with a candle to look in on them. She would retire to her bedchamber, the house would be dark and quiet, and everyone would be asleep. Then he would leave for his post at George's tent.

The next thing John knew, light from the pale gray morning sky was filtering into the bedchamber. In spite of his good intentions, he had slept through the night.

He dressed hurriedly, raced downstairs, and ran as fast as he could to the encampment, where he could see George drilling a small group of volunteers.

There had been no raid, or George would not be there behaving as though everything was normal. Disappointed, John went home to complete his studies before he was called to breakfast.

It was that afternoon, just as the burgesses were adjourning for the session, that the raid took place. John, who saw crowds gathering at the Magazine, ran across the street to join them.

Theodorick Bland, a friend of George's, stood at the door to the Magazine, a stack of muskets beside him. As quickly as he could, he handed them out to anyone who claimed he needed a weapon.

"Theo! I need a gun!" John cried, and stretched out his hands.

Theodorick laughed. "These arms are not for children," he said.

John took a step back, embarrassed. There was no point in arguing with Theo that he was no longer a child. "Are these from the palace?" he asked.

Another friend of George's, James Monroe, arrived in a cart piled high with more pistols, muskets, and swords. "We've taken at least two hundred pistols and muskets!" he shouted.

John set off for the palace, running until he got a stitch in his side. He arrived at the open gate gasping for breath and saw that the doors to the entrance hall were open wide. As he approached, he noticed that the gleaming wood-paneled walls were bare of the arms that had hung there, and the ceiling bore only the hooks and fasteners that had supported the muskets, pistols, and swords.

Peering into the entry hall from the next room, which John could see had also been stripped of arms, were some of the governor's slaves. Their eyes were wide and fearful.

George jumped down from a ladder that rested against one of the walls. He took two steps toward the door, then stopped and turned to the slaves. "You will come to no harm," he said gently. "I will make it known that you protested our entering the palace but we took the arms by force."

As George leaped down the steps of the palace clutching a last armful of weapons, John hurried to him. "George, give me a pistol," he said.

George smiled broadly. "Not for you, lad," he said. "What do you think Father would do to me?"

"A sword, then." John knew his brother was unable to hear him because a crowd had gathered, rushing toward him as he walked through the gates. People laughed and shouted out praise to George.

"That will show our fine governor!"

"Said we can't have the weapons from the palace, did he?"

"Good for you!"

John's disappointment at not being on hand for the raid and not being able to have a weapon of his own began to turn into pride in his brother, who was being hailed as a hero. John had to run to keep up with George's long stride all the way back to the Magazine.

John tried to defend George's actions to their father, but Mr. Nicholas was indignant. "All the young men who participated in the raid should be ashamed," he said. "Benjamin Harrison, Jr., James Monroe, Theodorick Bland . . . and George. Young men from fine families, educated, with a heritage of good manners . . . How could they have behaved like a pack of outlaws? Didn't they consider the effect their behavior would have on the entire colony?"

"Father, the colonists need those weapons," John said. "Now more men in Williamsburg will be able to defend themselves."

"And peaceful negotiations have come to an end."

"Not because of George, Father—" John began. He intended to remind his father that the governor himself had made peaceful negotiations impossible.

But Mr. Nicholas turned to leave the room, saying, "I have no time to listen to your defense of your brother. Suppose you spend your efforts where they will be most profitable—on your studies."

Five days later, Lady Dunmore and her children sailed for England on board the H.M.S. *Magdalen,* but Governor Dunmore remained on the *Fowey,* not intending to return to Williamsburg.

"He is sending his family away," Betsey reported. "And he's announced that he will no longer help Virginia. He will fight Virginians. Many of the governor's close supporters are leaving for England."

Mary said, "The governor's aide, Captain Foy, will not be missed. He is every bit as arrogant as Governor Dunmore. Sally's husband was told that Captain Foy laughed when he heard that Geo—um, that the arms had been taken from the palace. He made a rude comment about the young men who had taken them, then said they had taken only those in sight, not those that had been well hidden inside the palace."

"Then good riddance to him," Betsey said. She sighed, adding, "Edmund's father has booked passage on a ship that will leave in three weeks. He is taking with him everyone in the family but Edmund, who refuses to go. Edmund told me that his sisters have cried and pleaded. They do not want to leave Virginia and go to England to live, but their father will not change his mind."

"Dear Betsey," Mrs. Nicholas said sympathetically. "I know this is hard for both you and Edmund."

For Edmund, perhaps, John thought, but not for Betsey. He was certain that John Randolph would prove to be a cranky, hard-to-please father-in-law.

"Edmund has applied for the position of aide to General Washington," Betsey said. "If he is accepted, he will no longer be in Williamsburg." She burst into tears.

John felt sorry for Betsey, but he left his mother and Mary to soothe her. As he walked outside in the warm summer sun, the sharp fragrance of heliotrope tickled his nose, and he rubbed it. Carefully, he thought over what Mary had said about Captain Foy. Could it be true that arms were hidden somewhere in the palace? Why would the captain have made that statement if they were not? John didn't know.

But there was one thing of which he was completely certain. George should be told what Captain Foy had said.

George listened intently as John repeated the captain's remark. He rubbed his chin and pursed his lips as he thought. "So there may be a hidden cache of arms," he finally said. "That is interesting news. Thank you, John, for relaying it to me."

John looked up at George, waiting. Finally, he said, "Well? Will you and your friends visit the palace again?"

George made a slight bow and grinned. "I'm afraid there is no one in residence to receive us socially."

"Oh, George, you know what I mean," John said. "Are you going to plan another raid?"

"That remains to be seen," George answered.

John took a deep breath, making a wish for the answer he wanted. "If you do, will you take me?"

"Absolutely not," George answered.

John didn't argue with him. It didn't matter what George said. John was determined that this time, he would be on hand.

Chapter Ten

Later that day, volunteers from New Kent arrived to help guard Williamsburg, responding to Peyton Randolph's call. And two days later, on June 30, extra volunteers from New Kent and York arrived to become part of the guard. Most of them set up their campsites in Waller's Grove, at the eastern end of Williamsburg.

John could see that George had his hands full working with his own company and some new recruits who had joined to help guard the Magazine. But he knew his brother, and he watched that familiar distant look come into his eyes. George was planning to do something when the time was right. Excitement made John's heart beat faster. He knew George was making plans for another raid.

121

In early July, Mr. Nicholas came cheerfully to the table at suppertime. "A messenger from Philadelphia brought word that John Dickinson's petition to King George for reconciliation was adopted by Congress on July fifth," he said.

"Another petition to the king, Father?" Mary asked. "What good will it do?"

"It will do a great deal of good if the king sees our eagerness to reconcile. It is a well-written petition. It repeats the grievances of the colonists, but it also offers an olive branch, making clear our attachment to the king and our earnest hope to avoid further hostilities."

"I hope it will be well received by His Majesty," Mrs. Nicholas said.

John had no such hopes. The king and Parliament were showing no interest in working out the problems peacefully. With the British army fighting the Continental Army in the northern colonies, and Lord Dunmore's departure from Williamsburg, how could anyone—including his father and Mr. Dickinson—imagine that the king and Parliament would be sympathetic to the colonies' proposal?

John and Robert visited George's company the next morning. Beverley had returned. He looked a little thinner and a little paler, and a clean white cloth was wrapped around his head. "They told me you saved my life," he solemnly said to John. "I am grateful to you."

John felt his face grow warm, and he ducked his head. "It was the doctor who saved you. I only did what I could to stop the bleeding." He shuddered, remembering vividly how Beverley had lain on the ground as if he were dead, blood oozing down his chin and neck into the soil.

"Well, now I'm fit enough to tend to my duties," Beverley said cheerfully. "Will you lads drill with us today?"

John looked to each side, where men were moving into formation. "No," he said. "I'm looking for my brother George."

"He's not here," Beverley answered. "I saw him leave close to an hour ago."

John stiffened. "Where was he going?"

Beverley grinned. "I'm just a lowly foot soldier. He's not about to tell me his plans."

"Do you know which direction he took?" John persisted.

"He left in Mr. Bland's carriage. Mr. Monroe was with him." Beverley thought a moment. "Far as I remember, they went west—toward Palace green."

"Thanks," John cried out. He grabbed Robert's arm, spinning him around, and began running. "Come on, Robert! Hurry!"

"Where are we going?" Robert shouted as he ran to catch up.

"To find George!" John called.

As they neared the palace, they slowed, gulping air to catch their breaths.

The street was empty except for two carts parked outside the gates. No one was in sight, not even a groom to tend the horses. Beyond, the great doors to the entrance hall of the palace were shut.

"George isn't here," Robert said. "Not even the governor is here."

"Remember when George and his friends took the armaments from the palace?" John asked.

"Of course I remember," Robert answered.

John lowered his voice. "Well, they didn't get them all. The governor's aide, Captain Foy, told some people that there was a cache of arms still hidden in the palace. He laughed because George and his friends hadn't known about them."

"So you think George will come back to find the arms?"

John glanced at the west side yard of the palace, where he could see a group of slaves clustered together, concern on their faces. "I think George is here now," he said.

As he ran up the steps to the large front doors, he could see that one was slightly ajar. Pushing it open, he poked his head through. "George?" he called. "Are you in here?"

Theodorick Bland appeared so suddenly that John jumped, letting out a yelp of surprise.

His voice low, Theo ordered, "Leave immediately, John! Go home!"

John stubbornly stood his ground. He wouldn't allow Theo to tell him what to do. It was George he had come to see. "Robert and I are here to help search for the hidden arms," he said.

Theo narrowed his eyes and studied John. "Whom have you told about this?"

"No one. Only George. I told him what Captain Foy said about your missing the arms that were hidden. That's why he's here."

Taking a step closer, Theo said, "John, you and Robert *must* leave. The armaments in the palace belong to the people of Virginia, so if we find them we can take them. But if we don't find them, or if their existence is only a rumor, we could be arrested for trespassing. I'm certain that you and Robert would not like to spend your days locked in the gaol."

John thought a moment. He wanted to be part of the search, but he hated the idea of being locked inside the Public Gaol.

Without waiting for an answer, Theo grabbed John's shoulders, turned him around, and gave him a gentle push. "Leave," he said. "Your remaining here can only hinder our search. You want to help your brother, don't you?"

"Yes," John said. He slowly walked down the steps to join Robert, who stared at John with wide eyes.

"You heard what Theo said, didn't you?" John asked.

Robert nodded. "We should do what Theo told us to do. I don't want to be locked in the gaol."

As they walked slowly down Palace Street, John suddenly stopped in shock. Coming toward them at a brisk stride was John Randolph, Edmund's father. Long a friend of Governor Dunmore and often his visitor, he seemed to be headed directly for the Governor's Palace.

"He'll find George and his friends there," John whispered to Robert. "We must give George time to find the guns! We must stop Mr. Randolph!"

"We can't do that. Perhaps he's been sent there by Governor Dunmore to get something the governor needs."

"We must do something to stop him!" John repeated. He frantically searched for an answer, and finally, one came to him. "Robert," he said, "whatever I do, agree with me. Say whatever comes into your head. Help me!"

Mr. Randolph had almost reached them when John clutched his throat, making terrible gagging noises.

Mr. Randolph stopped, staring at John, who fell at his feet, twitching and gagging.

"Is the lad having a fit?" Mr. Randolph asked.

"Yes, sir," Robert answered. "And there's no one to help him . . . but *you*."

From the corners of his eyes, John could see Mr. Randolph glance to each side. "Where is his mother?"

"At home on Francis Street at the corner of South England Street," Robert said.

"But that is the home of Robert Carter Nicholas!"

"That's right, sir. This is his son John."

John squeezed his eyes tight and made a terrible noise in his throat.

"I am alone. He is large. I cannot carry him," Mr. Randolph began, but John, groaning loudly, began to struggle to his feet.

"I think he can walk if we help him," Robert said.

John leaned against Mr. Randolph and moaned pitifully.

"Very well," Mr. Randolph said. "We cannot leave the lad without assistance."

Mr. Randolph bent over, pulling one of John's

arms across his shoulder. "You take his other arm," Mr. Randolph instructed Robert. "We will manage to get him home, where he can be cared for."

It was a slow trip. John stumbled, sometimes dragging a foot. He guessed that it took nearly twenty minutes to cover the distance to Duke of Gloucester Street.

They had no sooner turned the corner when a cart came up behind them. It clattered past, the horses pulling it at full speed. Behind it raced another.

"Foolish young men!" Mr. Randolph snapped. "There is no need to drive in such a reckless fashion."

But John had recognized his brother on the first vehicle, and he had seen the glint of polished metal. They had found the hidden supply of arms!

He straightened and pulled his arm from Mr. Randolph's shoulder. "Thank you for your help, sir," he said.

John Randolph took a step back in surprise. "Your fit has passed? You are well again?"

"My thanks to you, sir. All is now well," John answered.

"Perhaps I should still accompany you to your home." Mr. Randolph looked doubtful.

"I'm greatly obliged to you, sir," John said with a bow, "but I am now perfectly well." A strong wave of guilt swept through him. In spite of his being loyal to the British government and no friend to John's father, Mr. Randolph had been kind enough to help. When he reached the palace, he would discover from the slaves what had happened and know he had been tricked.

But John reminded himself that John Randolph was a friend of Governor Dunmore, who had announced his decision to lay waste to Virginia. *I have no regrets,* John told himself. He had saved George and his friends from being arrested. By giving them the time to find the hidden arms, he had also helped Virginia.

John, with Robert beside him, set off at a run for the Magazine.

Chapter Eleven

As word spread about the second raid, George became a hero to the people of Williamsburg. But Mr. Nicholas made it clear that George was not a hero to him.

John was upstairs that evening when he heard George arrive. His voice and their father's almost immediately rose in anger.

With a groan, John got out of his high-post bed, lit his candle, and crept down the stairs, dressed only in his shirt. The voices came now from his father's study, so John padded barefoot across the hall, pausing at the door to the room.

"Father," John said quietly.

Mr. Nicholas didn't seem to hear him. Instead, he gripped the back of his chair, leaning toward George in his anger. "How can we reach a peaceful settlement with the Crown if you and your friends continue these bold acts that anger the authorities?"

"Father?" John said more loudly.

Mr. Nicholas didn't answer. He was intent on his argument with George.

"Can you not see you will never reach a peaceful settlement?" George insisted. "The king will never accept your petition."

"We do not know that. He must be given time to respond," Mr. Nicholas said.

John took a deep breath and strode into the room, stepping between his brother and father. "I pray you both," he said, "listen to what I have to say."

As both Mr. Nicholas and George turned to look at John with surprise, he continued, "I played a part in that raid, Father."

He went on to tell how he had passed on to George what Captain Foy had said about the hidden arms. And he described what he had done to draw John Randolph away from the palace so that George and his friends wouldn't be caught before the arms were found.

"Brother," George said gently, "I am grateful for what you did, but you need not try to defend my actions to Father or share the blame."

Stubbornly, John shook his head. "There should

be no blame. Those guns belong to the people of Virginia. The governor had no right to hide them."

"There are legal ways of obtaining—" Mr. Nicholas began, but John interrupted.

"Father," he said, "even though you didn't like it, Governor Dunmore was right to lump you and your friends with Patrick Henry and George and his friends, because all of you wish the same thing— your rights and liberty."

Mr. Nicholas's eyes opened wide in surprise. "Surely you don't think that—"

"Pray hear me out," John insisted. "You consider me only a child, but even as a child it is plain to me that it will be necessary to fight to gain the liberty that we deserve. You have tried to reach this goal your way. George has tried his. But it is only fair to recognize that you are both after the same results, and now it's time for you to work together."

Mr. Nicholas slowly sank into his chair and said, "I have tried so hard to avoid our colonies' becoming involved in a revolt against Great Britain."

George rested a hand on his father's shoulder. "And you are highly respected for the work you have done."

Looking up at George, Mr. Nicholas said, "We will pay a high price for liberty. Many of us will lose property, businesses, investments . . . but far worse, many will lose family members. . . . The many sacrifices . . ."

As he broke off, George said, "Father, liberty is so valuable to all men that we cannot count the price. We must work together to win it, no matter what it takes."

John waited, holding his breath, until his father answered, "You are right, Son. I agree."

A slight movement in the hall caught John's eye. He turned to see Samson passing the open doorway. John suddenly thought of Samson and Titus and the rest of the family's slaves with a burst of sympathy. He no longer feared their leaving. He knew that they, too, would do whatever they could to gain the freedom they believed they deserved.

John left the study and climbed the stairs. He didn't know what Governor Dunmore would do next. He had no idea what King George III and the members of Parliament might decide. Perhaps Dunmore *would* free the slaves. Perhaps the volunteer companies *would* do battle with the royal marines. It was even possible that one day soon, the united colonies would be at war with Great Britain.

John was only certain of one thing—that whatever took place in the future, his family would see it through together. Their goals were the same. They were no longer a divided family.

Epilogue

Mrs. Otts leaned back, smoothing her apron. "King George III did not read what historians have called the Olive Branch Petition sent to him by Congress. As a matter of fact, he even refused to receive it."

"Why didn't he want to cooperate with the colonists?" Keisha asked. "I think Robert Carter Nicholas's idea of trying to solve things peacefully was a good one."

Stewart didn't give Mrs. Otts time to answer. He said, "I think there were too many people between the colonists and the king—people like Governor Dunmore, who seemed to want to hurt Virginians, not help them."

"Hey, you know what?" Chip said. "The Americans who protested the unfair taxes and laws didn't want to stop being British. They just wanted to be given their rights. If the British authorities had been reasonable, the history of our country might have turned out to be very different."

" 'Tis true," Mrs. Otts said, "but instead, on August 23, 1775, King George III issued a proclamation declaring the colonies to be in a state of rebellion."

Halim spoke up. "I have a question, Mrs. Otts. Did Governor Dunmore ever free the slaves?"

"That he did," Mrs. Otts answered. " 'Twas on November 7, 1775, that he wrote the proclamation, but he waited to issue it until November 15, after the British had won a small military victory. He declared martial law and freed all slaves belonging to 'rebels'—patriots, we call them—who, as he put it, 'are able and willing to bear Arms,' and would join His Majesty's forces. Samson and Titus left the Nicholas home and joined the British."

"How about Betty?" Lori asked.

"Betty and her daughter, Diana, remained with the Nicholas family."

Lori hugged her knees. "Do you know what happened to John Nicholas and his family during the Revolutionary War?" she asked.

Mrs. Otts nodded. "Yes, I do. Peyton Randolph returned to the Continental Congress in September 1775, at which point Robert Carter Nicholas succeeded him as president of the Virginia Convention. That was the extralegal body of officials who ran the colony while the House of Burgesses was not in session during the approach to the Revolution.

"Mr. Nicholas chaired the committee to appoint officers for his district's militia and battalion of minutemen." She smiled. "You may be pleased to learn that among the committee's appointments were George, given the rank of captain, and Beverley Dickson, promoted to lieutenant.

"In 1777, for safety's sake, Robert Carter Nicholas moved his family to a plantation in Hanover County to live.

"The Colonial Williamsburg Department of Historical Research has records of all the children in Robert Carter Nicholas's family who married, conducted business, or sold property for a number of years *after* the war. That includes the youngest child, Philip Norborne Nicholas, who was born on February 27, 1776. Therefore, we know they survived the Revolution."

Smiling, Lori said, "I'm glad—just as John was—that his family wasn't divided during the war. When you told us that Edmund Randolph's parents, brothers, and sisters left for England, it made me feel sad for him."

"War is always sad," Keisha said.

"But out of the protests came a full-scale revolution and a brand-new independent country," Stewart said. "The colonists were no longer British subjects. They were free."

"Most of them," Mrs. Otts said. "As for the slaves—well, that's something I'm sure you'll learn much more about as you continue to study American history."

She smiled. "And any time you wish to learn more about the colonial period in Virginia history, come back to visit me. You'll always be able to find me in Market Square."

Author's Note

Detailed material about Robert Carter Nicholas can be found in the Colonial Williamsburg archives because he was one of eighteenth-century Williamsburg's leading citizens. There are also many historic notations about his son George, who— among other things—helped organize two raids on the Governor's Palace to remove the many pistols, swords, and muskets stored there and distribute them to the people of Williamsburg.

It was easy for me to imagine the arguments that might have taken place between father and son in the Nicholas household. But Robert Carter Nicholas had other children, and I wondered how they would feel about the conflict taking place in their own home. I wanted to use one of them to tell this story about Williamsburg in 1775. Whom should I choose?

There were three daughters. One of them—Sarah "Sally" Norton—was married and lived in her own home with her husband, John Hatley Norton. I'm sure her concern was more for her own children than for her brother's skirmishes with their father. I was glad to discover Sarah Norton again. She was the same Sarah Norton who had recognized Maria Rind's plight (which I wrote about in *Maria's Story: 1773*) and had rescued her by asking a good friend, Frances Randolph, to take Maria into her household. Sarah was not close enough to the situation in the Nicholas household. I didn't choose Sarah.

I didn't choose Betsey, either. Betsey married Edmund Randolph in 1776. We don't know exactly when Edmund began courting Betsey, but they were born on the same day and had been friends since they were very young. Since the spring and summer of 1775 was a difficult time for Edmund, with his father renouncing Virginia and taking his wife and children to England, I'm fairly sure Edmund would have relied on Betsey's friendship and comfort. It would have been only natural for Betsey's main interest to be Edmund, not her younger brother.

Mary, at sixteen, would have been a romantic and willing ally to her sister, who had chosen to fall in love with the son of a man their father heartily disliked. If George and their father disagreed, that was nothing new to her. George had always been impulsive and quick to speak out. Mary wasn't my choice.

Lewis was only eight years old in 1775. He must have admired what his big brother was doing, but I didn't think he was old enough yet to try to pattern himself after George. Not Lewis.

Wilson Cary was fourteen, but as I read about the family, I discovered that when they were grown, Lewis lost his farm because of Wilson's "financial imprudence." Writers need to like their main characters to enjoy writing about them, and I decided that I didn't like Wilson as much as I should if I were going to write from his viewpoint. My main character wouldn't be Wilson.

That left John, and I knew immediately that John was the perfect choice to tell the story. At the age of eleven, he would have been old enough to be well aware of what was taking place between Great Britain and the American colonies. And he would have been torn by his loyalties to both his father and his much-loved eldest brother.

I knew also that Robert Carter Nicholas would have been deeply concerned and involved with the political situation, so much so that his many duties would have kept him from spending the time with John that John so badly needed and asked for.

Research told me only that John grew up, married a woman named Ann Lawson, moved to New York, and died in 1819 at the age of fifty-five. There was nothing to show that John was present when Beverley Dickson and at least two other young men were wounded by the spring-loaded gun set at the Magazine. And there is no record that John helped George remain undetected at the Governor's Palace until the hidden arms were found. There was no information about the details of John's boyhood.

But wouldn't an active eleven-year-old boy do everything he could to help his brother? And wouldn't he also try his best to prove that he could help in the cause for liberty? I was sure that John would not have allowed himself to be left out of the Magazine raid or the raids on the Governor's Palace.

The episodes of the spring-loaded gun and the two raids on the palace were true and took place much the way I have described them. Involving John in them was *my* choice.

Again, I enjoyed doing a little detective work. In my research, I learned only that George and his friends suspected there was a hidden cache of arms in the palace. Someone had to give rise to that suspicion. Someone had to know the information and perhaps leak it. The logical suspect was Captain Edward Foy, who was aide to Lord Dunmore and would have been the most likely one to share this kind of secret. Before Foy left for England, he made it clear he disliked Dunmore and spoke against him bitterly. It was highly possible that Foy gave away the secret information about the arms.

On September 1, 1775, King George III refused to receive the final petition of the Continental Congress, and on November 10, the final petition was rejected by the British House of Lords.

Even before our delegates to the Continental Congress in Philadelphia adopted the Declaration of Independence on July 4, 1776, our colonies were at war—a war that didn't end officially until September 3, 1783, when Great Britain signed the Treaty of Paris, ending the American Revolution.

However, with communication as slow as it was in the 1700s, official word of the ratification of the peace treaty between Great Britain and the United States of America didn't reach Virginians until five months later—on February 3, 1784, less than a month after John's twentieth birthday.

Had he been able to serve his new country in the Continental Army as he had wanted to do? I think he had. Do you?

About Williamsburg

The story of Williamsburg, the capital of eighteenth-century Virginia, began more than seventy-five years before the thirteen original colonies became the United States in 1776.

Williamsburg was the colony's second capital. Jamestown, the first permanent English settlement in North America, was the first. Jamestown stood on a swampy peninsula in the James River, and over the years, people found it an unhealthy place to live. They also feared that ships sailing up the river could attack the town.

In 1699, a year after the Statehouse at Jamestown burned down for the fourth time, Virginians decided to move the capital a few miles away, to a place known

The Capitol at Williamsburg

as Middle Plantation. On high ground between two rivers, Middle Plantation was a healthier and safer location that was already home to several of Virginia's leading citizens.

Middle Plantation was also the home of the College of William and Mary, today one of Virginia's most revered institutions. The college received its charter from King William III and Queen Mary II of England in 1693. Its graduates include two of our nation's first presidents: Thomas Jefferson and James Monroe.

The new capital's name was changed to Williamsburg in honor of King William. Like the Colony of Virginia, Williamsburg grew during the eighteenth century. Government officials and their families arrived. Taverns opened for business, and merchants and artisans settled in. Much of the heavy labor and domestic work was performed by African Americans, most of them slaves, although a few were free. By the eve of the American Revolution, nearly two thousand people—roughly half of them white and half of them black—lived in Williamsburg.

The Revolutionary War and Its Leaders

The formal dates of the American Revolution are 1775 to 1783, but the problems between the thirteen original colonies and Great Britain, their mother country, began in 1765, when Parliament enacted the Stamp Act.

England was in debt from fighting the Seven Years War (called the French and Indian War in the colonies) and believed that the colonists should help pay the debt. The colonists were stunned. They considered themselves English and believed they had the same political rights as people living in England. These rights included being taxed *only* by an elected body, such as each colony's legislature. Now a body in which they were not represented, Parliament, was taxing them.

A reenactment of Virginia legislators debating the Stamp Act

All thirteen colonies protested, and the Stamp Act was repealed in 1766. Over the next nine years, however, Great Britain imposed other taxes and enacted other laws that the colonists believed infringed on their rights. Finally, in 1775, the Second Continental Congress, made up of representatives from twelve of the colonies, established an army. The following year, the Congress (now with representatives from all thirteen colonies) declared independence from Great Britain.

The Revolutionary War was the historical event that ensured Williamsburg's place in American history. Events that happened there and the people who participated in them helped form the values on which the United States was founded. Virginians meeting in Williamsburg helped lead the thirteen colonies to independence.

In fact, Americans first declared independence in the Capitol in Williamsburg. There, on May 15, 1776, the colony's leaders declared Virginia's full freedom from England. In a unanimous vote, they also instructed the colony's representatives to the Continental Congress to propose that the Congress "declare the United Colonies free and independent states absolved from all allegiances to or dependence upon the Crown or Parliament of Great Britain."

Three weeks later, Richard Henry Lee, one of Virginia's delegates, stood before the Congress and proposed independence. His action led directly to the writing of the Declaration of Independence. The Congress adopted the Declaration on July 2 and signed it two days later. The United States of America was born.

Williamsburg served as a training ground for

three noteworthy patriots: George Washington, Thomas Jefferson, and Patrick Henry. Each arrived in Williamsburg as a young man, and there each matured into a statesman.

In 1752, George Washington, who later led the American forces to victory over the British in the Revolutionary War and became our nation's first president, came to Williamsburg at the age of nineteen. He soon began a career in the military, which led to a seat in Virginia's legislature, the House of Burgesses. He served as a burgess for sixteen years—negotiating legislation, engaging in political discussions, and building social and political relationships. These experiences helped mold him into one of America's finest political leaders.

Patrick Henry, who would go on to become the first governor of the Commonwealth of Virginia as well as a powerful advocate for the Bill of Rights, first traveled to Williamsburg in 1760 to obtain a law license. Only twenty-three years old, he barely squeaked through the exam. Five years later, as a first-time burgess, he led Virginia's opposition to the Stamp Act. For the next eleven years, Henry's talent as a speaker—including his now famous Caesar-Brutus speech and the immortal cry, "Give me liberty or give me death!"—rallied Virginians to the patriots' cause.

Thomas Jefferson, who later wrote the Declaration of Independence, succeeded Patrick Henry as the governor of Virginia, and became the third president of the United States, arrived in Williamsburg in 1760 at the age of seventeen to attend the College of William and Mary. As the cousin of Peyton Randolph, the respected Speaker of the House of Burgesses, Jefferson was immediately welcomed by Williamsburg society. He became a lawyer and was elected a burgess in 1769. In his very first session, the royal governor closed the legislature because it had protested the Townshend Acts. The burgesses moved the meeting to the Raleigh Tavern, where they drew up an agreement to boycott British goods.

Jefferson, Henry, and Washington each signed the agreement. In the years that followed, all three men supported the patriots' cause and the nation that grew out of it.

Williamsburg Then and Now

Williamsburg in the eighteenth century was a vibrant American town. Thanks largely to the vision of the Reverend Dr. W.A.R. Goodwin, rector of Bruton Parish Church at the opening of the twentieth century, its vitality can still be experienced today. The generosity of philanthropist John D. Rockefeller, Jr., made it possible to restore Williamsburg to its eighteenth-century glory. Original colonial buildings

The Reverend Dr. W.A.R. Goodwin with John D. Rockefeller, Jr.

were acquired and carefully returned to their eighteenth-century appearance. Later houses and buildings were torn down and replaced by carefully researched reconstructions, most built on original eighteenth-century foundations. Rockefeller gave the project both money and enthusiastic support for more than thirty years.

Today, the Historic Area of Williamsburg is both a museum and a living city. The restored buildings, antique furnishings, and costumed interpreters can help you create a picture of the past in your mind's eye. The Historic Area is operated by the Colonial Williamsburg Foundation, a nonprofit educational organization staffed by historians, interpreters, actors, administrators, numerous people behind the scenes, and many volunteers.

Williamsburg is a living reminder of our country's past and a guide to its future; it shows us where we have been and can give us clues about where we may be going. Though the stories of the people who lived in the eighteenth-century Williamsburg may seem very different from our lives in the twenty-first century, the heart of the stories remains the same. We created a nation based on new ideas about liberty, independence, and democracy. The Colonial Williamsburg: Young Americans books are about individuals who may not have experienced these principles in their own lives, but whose lives foreshadowed changes for the generations that followed. People like the smart and capable Ann McKenzie in *Ann's Story: 1747*, who struggled to reconcile her interest in medicine with society's expectations for an eighteenth-century woman. People like the brave Caesar in *Caesar's Story: 1759*, who

152

struggled in silence against the institution of slavery that gripped his people, his family, and himself. While some of these lives evoke painful memories of

A scene from Colonial Williamsburg today

our country's history, they are a part of that history nonetheless and cannot be forgotten. These stories form the foundation of our country. The people in them are the unspoken heroes of our time.

Childhood in Eighteenth-Century Virginia

If you traveled back in time to Virginia in the 1700s, some things would probably seem familiar to you. Colonial children played some of the same games that children play today: blindman's buff, hopscotch, leapfrog, and hide-and-seek. Girls had dolls, boys flew kites, and both boys and girls might play with puzzles and read.

You might be surprised, however, at how few toys even well-to-do children owned. Adults and children in the 1700s owned far fewer things than we do today, not only fewer toys but also less furniture and clothing. And the books children read were either educational or taught them how to behave properly, such as *Aesop's Fables* and the *School of Manners.*

Small children dressed almost alike back then. Boys and girls in prosperous families wore gowns

(dresses) similar to the ones older girls and women wore. Less well-to-do white children and enslaved children wore shifts, which were much like our nightgowns. Both black and white boys began wearing pants when they were between five and seven years old.

Boys and girls in colonial Virginia began doing chores when they were six or seven, probably the same age at which *you* started doing chores around the house. But their chores included tasks such as toting kindling, grinding corn with a mortar and pestle, and turning a spit so that meat would roast evenly over the fire.

These chores were done by both black and white children. Many enslaved children also began working in the fields at this age. They might pick worms off tobacco, carry water to older workers, hoe, or pull weeds. However, they usually were not expected to do as much work as the adults.

As black and white children grew older, they were assigned more and sometimes harder chores. Few children of either race went to school. Those who did usually came from prosperous white families, although there were some charity schools. Some middling (middle-class) and gentry (upper-class) children studied at home with tutors. Other white children learned from their mothers and fathers to read, write, and do simple arithmetic. But not all white children were taught these skills, and very few enslaved children learned them.

When they were ten, eleven, or twelve years old, children began preparing in earnest for adulthood.

Boys from well-to-do families got a university education at the College of William and Mary in Williamsburg or at a university in England. Their advanced studies prepared them to manage the plantations they inherited or to become lawyers and important government officials. Many did all three things.

Many middle-class boys and some poorer ones became apprentices. An apprentice agreed to work for a master for several years, usually until the apprentice turned twenty-one. The master agreed to teach the apprentice his trade or profession, to ensure that he learned to read and write, and, usually, to feed, clothe,

An apprentice with the master cabinetmaker

and house him. Apprentices became apothecaries (druggist-doctors), blacksmiths, carpenters, coopers (barrel makers), founders (men who cast metals in a foundry), merchants, printers, shoemakers, silversmiths, store clerks, and wigmakers. Some girls, usually orphans with no families, also became apprentices. A girl apprentice usually lived with a family and worked as a domestic servant.

Most white girls, however, learned at home. Their mothers or other female relatives taught them the skills they would need to manage their households after they married—such as cooking, sewing, knitting, cleaning, doing the laundry, managing domestic slaves, and caring for ailing family members. Some middle-class and most gentry girls also learned music, dance, embroidery, and sometimes French. Formal education for girls of all classes, however, was usually limited to reading, writing, and arithmetic.

Enslaved children also began training for adulthood when they were ten to twelve years old. Some boys and girls worked in the house and learned to be domestic slaves. Others worked in the fields. Some boys learned a trade.

Because masters had to pay taxes on slaves who were sixteen years old or older, slaves were expected to do a full day's work when they turned sixteen, if not sooner. White boys, however, usually were not considered adults until they reached the age of twenty-one. White girls were considered to be adults when they turned twenty-one or married, whichever came first.

Enslaved or free black boys watching tradesmen saw wood

When we look back, we see many elements of colonial childhood that are familiar to us—the love of toys and games, the need to help the family around the house, and the task of preparing for adulthood. However, it is interesting to compare the days of a colonial child to the days of a child today, and to see all the ways in which life has changed for children over the years.

Revolution in Eighteenth-Century Virginia

The conflicts between John's father, Robert Carter Nicholas, and his oldest brother, George, paralleled the larger political debate in 1775. Virginians faced complex decisions as the colony moved toward independence. Some had been unhappy with the Crown since just after the end of the French and Indian War. By 1760, Americans began to worry that the British constitution was not protecting their rights as British citizens, including personal security, personal liberty, and private property. The British government's ideas about managing the colonies were different from some Americans' ideas about liberty and their rights as citizens. Virginians had

Two gentlemen debate the future of the Virginia colony.

to sort out where their loyalties lay—with the Crown or with the colonies.

English, Scots, Irish, Welsh, Africans and African Americans, Native Americans, Germans, and other racial and ethnic groups all lived in Virginia. Within these varied groups, some were American patriots, some were loyalists, and some switched sides or remained undecided.

Many free Virginians wanted to break away from Great Britain. James Innes, an usher, or assistant teacher, at the College of William and Mary in Williamsburg, became captain of the Williamsburg volunteer militia. John and his friend Robert watched as James drilled young men for possible combat with British troops.

Loyalists believed in many of the same principles as patriots, but they believed that continued loyalty to the Crown was the best decision. Some Virginia loyalists such as John Randolph thought that war with the mother country was such a reckless and misguided course of action that they left Virginia and moved to England.

Recently freed African American slaves train with British soldiers.

In most cases, family members followed the choice of the head of the household. Edmund Randolph, who courted John's sister Betsey, did not share his father's loyalty to the king's cause and remained in America as aide-de-camp to General Washington. Two of the Nicholas slaves, Samson and Titus, discussed whether to accept Governor Dunmore's offer to join the British and go free. Slaves who joined the British army were also fighting for freedom, although their rebellion was against Virginia masters, not royal authority. Slaves who stayed with their Virginia masters remained in a system that saw them as property.

Some Virginians sat out the war, never committing themselves to one side or the other. Others, such as Williamsburg printer William Hunter and lawyer James Hubard, switched sides.

Economics was a deciding factor for many. Merchants dependent on commerce with Great Britain stood to lose by colonial embargoes and by war. Milliner Catherine Rathell closed her business and boarded a ship for Great Britain. Other tradespeople

A Native American assists soldiers.

expected to prosper from a conflict. James Anderson, blacksmith, and Peter Powell, wheelwright, expanded their operations to supply the American army.

Native Americans chose sides during the war, basing their decisions on the outcome they believed would best serve their group's interests.

When Virginians were choosing whether to support revolution, they took beliefs and principles as well as family loyalty and personal gain into account. *John's Story: 1775* depicts the turmoil the Nicholas family—and all Virginians—faced when deciding for or against revolution in the year 1775.

Colonial Williamsburg Staff

Recipe for Queen's Cake

John's sister Betsey served coffee and queen's cake to women guests in the parlor after a formal dinner. Although colonial Virginians preferred tea, the Nicholases and their friends supported the boycott of tea established in mid-1774, and so drank coffee. With help from an adult, you can make queen's cake for your friends using the following recipe.

1 cup butter
1 cup sugar
5 eggs
1 teaspoon lemon extract
1 teaspoon orange extract

2 cups plus 1 tablespoon all-purpose flour
1/2 teaspoon baking powder
1/2 teaspoon cinnamon
2 cups currants

All the ingredients should be at room temperature. Grease well and lightly flour a 9¼ x 5¼ x 2¾-inch loaf pan. Cream the butter and sugar. Add the eggs, 1 at a time, beating well after each addition. Add the lemon and orange extracts. Sift 2 cups of the flour with the baking powder and cinnamon. Gradually add the flour mixture to the egg mixture. Dust the currants with the remaining 1 tablespoon of flour so that they do not sink to the bottom of the mixture. Fold the currants into the mixture. Bake in a pre-heated 325° F oven for 1 hour and 20 minutes or until done. Cool in the pan for 10 minutes before turning out onto a rack. Slice thinly.

From *Recipes from the Raleigh Tavern Bake Shop*, published by the Colonial Williamsburg Foundation

About the Author

Joan Lowery Nixon is the acclaimed author of more than a hundred books for young readers. She has served as president of the Mystery Writers of America and as regional vice president of the Southwest Chapter of that society. She is the only four-time winner of the Edgar Allan Poe Best Juvenile Mystery Award given by the Mystery Writers of America and is also a two-time winner of the Golden Spur Award for best juvenile Western, for two of the novels in her Orphan Train Adventures series.

Joan Lowery Nixon and her husband live in Houston.